DOUBLE FEATURE

p r e s e n t s

Que Sera Sera

Presented in state-of-the-art SepiaTone®

cover art
Paul "PJ" Johnson

design
Madi Quinn

contributing writers
Madi Quinn
DS Vernon
S.N. Humphreys

managing editors
DS Vernon
S.N. Humphreys

director of programming
W.P. Quigley

ASCENDENT

Table of Contents

WELCOME!

Welcome to the show!
Tonight we begin with the aptly titled short, Imposter Syndrome, by DS Vernon. Will our fledgling protagonist live up to the bar he has set himself? Can he compare to those whom he idolizes? Is he, in fact, on the road to becoming exactly who he says he is?

Next up, the first of two glimpses into the many lives of Grace Moore, the astounding, confounding, and downright horrifying, The Amazing Half Girl.

Then we come to our second short, Sleep, from the twisted mind of our own Madi Quinn, which asks us to travel down the rabbit hole to witness another becoming. This time a young girl channels the meager gifts she's been given into a bloody rebirth right before your very eyes.

And then, fair reader, onto our final attraction, The Girl Who Dreamed Too Loud. Who will Gracie Moore become when pushed to the brink of insanity? The only way to find out is to sit back, grab your preferred beverage and a tasty snack, and join us for Double Feature issue 3: Que Sera Sera.

- SN Humphreys
  June 2023

IMPOSTOR SYNDROME

DS VERNON

Impostor syndrome is a psychological occurrence in which an individual doubts their skills, talents, or accomplishmen[ts] and has a persistent internalized fear of being exposed as a fraud. Despite external evidence of their competence, tho[se] experiencing this phenomenon do not believe they deserve their success or luck.

What the fuck am I supposed to do with a name like Toby Leinhorn? This doesn't strike fear into the hearts of, well, anyone. I don't even have a middle name. Lazy mother of mine. All the greats had their middle names on full display. John *Wayne* Gacy, Henry *Lee* Lucas. Or at least they had more impressive names like Richard Ramirez or Jeffrey Dahmer. These names all hit with some impact whether you know them or not. Toby has no impact. A background character. Passive. I sound like an accountant. I *am* an accountant. I suppose I could change my name, but honestly how desperate and pathetic would that be? God, who does that? No, I'll have to do things so impactful that I get a nickname out of it. Nobody knows Dennis Rader, but they damn well know "The BTK Killer" Bind, Torture, Kill. Who the hell is Albert Desalvo? No idea, but that Boston Strangler is a monster.

But that's its own problem, isn't it? To become a villain to these people that is so iconic, so mysterious, so elusive, that all they can do is come up with a descriptio[n]. Something to call me while they try to make sense of [it] all, like the Night Stalker or The Green River Killer. Or become something when it's all over, when they eventual[ly] figure it all out like The Milwaukee Cannibal or The Kil[ler] Clown. How does a schlub like me live up to that? Ho[w] does one reach such heights and become iconic?

And shouldn't I have a type? Gacy had a crawlspa[ce] under his house positively filled to the brim with boys th[at] he had shown the handcuff trick (spoiler alert: the trick [is] that they are real handcuffs). The Son of Sam really did[n't] like long haired brunettes (or at least his neighbor's d[og] really didn't like them). Jack the Ripper specifically to[ok] issue with prostitutes. My mom was kind of a bitch on[ce] in a while, but she was no Augusta Wilhelmine Gein a[nd] certainly didn't turn me into her little Eddie. I suppos[e I] don't have a type. I hate everybody. Is that going to ma[ke] this whole thing easier because I can just pick whoever

n I going to spiral into indecision like I always do when
ere are too many choices?

All this talk of choices and I have to wonder about
ailable opportunities. I'm not a party clown, so I won't
endearing myself to anybody that way. I am no Ted
ndy; I have all the charisma of a boiled egg. Nobody
chhikes anymore, so I won't be able to follow in the
ssive footsteps of Ed Kemper. I'll need to find my own
portunities or better yet, make them.

I guess all I can do is hope to not make a complete
ol of myself. I feel so out of place among these giants.
solute legends in the field. Masters who have splattered
ir names across history with body counts or pure
tality. I'm not sure I can compare. I feel like such a
ud. I want, no *need,* to show that I am no fraud. I will be
real deal. I will be a monster for the books of history
d horror.

I mean, it's not like I am a complete novice. I've
e this a few times. Most recently was last year. I was
a quiet road, late at night and I saw a car wreck. Two
ple in the front seat. A dumb twenty-something and his
friend. They were trapped after he took a turn too fast
connected with a pole. And as luck would have it the
y they were pinned, their cell phones were just out of
ch.

A piece of metal jutted out in front of the driver.
seat belt had stopped him from becoming completely
aled on it. I reached in and pushed the top of his body
ward. He didn't have the strength left to fight me and
ply whimpered as the metal pierced his chest. In
much the same way, the girl sat, half alive, with a shard
of god knows what stuck in her neck. If it had pierced
her windpipe, it was also holding it mostly shut. She took
ragged nasty breaths, but she was definitely still breathing.
I pushed the shard deeper and twisted ever so slightly.
There was a squeak like a deflating balloon and a lot more
blood. And then the breathing stopped. I drove away.

I followed the news of this for weeks. The police
suspected nothing. A tragic car accident. There was even a
bit of a tussle between the fathers over the boy's careless
driving getting the girl killed. I had gotten away with it.
Easily.

But really now, that wasn't all that impressive was
it? Sure I'd gotten away with it. But they were both already
trapped. Both half dead. This was nothing compared to the
true greats. Five points out of ten. Six maybe if I am being
generous and heavily crediting the fact that nobody knew
it was a murder.

Well, If I am going to do this, *and do it for real*, I
have to start somewhere. Since, as I said, I don't feel like
I have a type, I'll wait for somebody to piss me off. That
shouldn't take long. I'm absolutely filled to the brim with
hate and the slightest nudge should make me overflow. I
am always teetering on the brink of explosion. Just waiting
to spill that cup.

I don't know when the moment will come, but it
sure as shit will. Humanity is a vapid wasteland devoid
of anything worth giving a shit about. The only trees that
bloom here are twisted and gnarled, bearing the fruit of
ignorance and stupidity. These trees need to be clear-cut.

The fruit needs to be destroyed before it can drop seeds. Nobody else is going to do it.

Driving home from work, I am cut off by some lowlife in a shit box beater of a car. The hatred spills, but I catch it and promise to release it later. I follow the driver and pull up next to him at a stop. Dirty long hair. Nicotine-stained fingernails and teeth. He notices me staring and flips me off. Yes. You'll do.

I've never tailed anybody like some undercover fed, but I am doing my best now. I've dropped back behind him with a few cars between us, trying to remember all the shitty detective movies and cop shows I've seen. When he finally takes a turn onto a residential street, I pass the turn and then double back. It feels like a high-risk move that could cause me to lose him, but I need to be careful.

In the distance, I catch a glimpse of what I believe is his car pulling into a driveway. I park, still far away and wait. After about 20 minutes I drive past his house. Yes, it is his house. I see that shitbox. I drive down the road a ways and park again. The houses on this street are all spaced out with big yards. They are all falling apart and dilapidated. I've struck gold here. Nobody is going to be paying attention to shit.

I go to my trunk and start digging through what's there. I find a dark hooded sweatshirt. I zip it and put the hood up. What else? Why didn't I put a knife or something in here? Toolbox. Yes. The box cutter catches my eye at first but ultimately, seems too small. Wrench? No. Pliers? Intriguing, but no. Claw hammer? Now I'm in business. I walk my way up to his house, trying to be quiet and

inconspicuous. I have no idea what I am doing at this poiñ I'm making it up as I go. But I am going to show them a I am not a fraud. I can't be. I can't.

I'm not sure yet how I am going to get in. I figu I have to look around a bit first. I start peering throu windows. Some of them have curtains. Some are pull back. But it's difficult because they are as nicotine-stain as his long disgusting nails. I lean in closer hoping to ge better view through the stains somehow.

"Hey, asshole! What the fuck are you doing at window?!" the voice behind me screams.

I nearly jump out of my skin. But all at once I turning. I feel almost outside myself as the hammer con up. By the time I've fully turned to him, the hamn connects with the side of his face, right by his mouth. goes down hard, dropping the trash bag, the reason he out here.

Blood is pooling next to his mouth and he coug Teeth come out. He begins to sputter "Wha-wha- da f but my hammer returns and abruptly cuts off his questi In the next instant I am on top of him, a knee in his ch so he can't escape, though it was hardly necessary.

The hammer comes down again and again again. I find myself surprised and elated at the variance sounds as the hammer impacts different parts of his he The sides and top crunch and cave in sounding like a me falling to the floor, dull and juicy. The face snaps shar like cracking Christmas walnuts. Soon enough though, whole thing sounds like tenderizing chicken cutlets, v blunt slapping. Bone and blood spray and leak and dar swing until I can no longer breathe.

I stand up and gaze down at my work. Moonlight catches on the blood, making the driveway glimmer.

I tilt my head back towards the sky, closing my eyes and basking in the moment. I feel the blood dripping down the sides of my face. It goes past my jaw, down my neck and into my shirt. So pure and wonderful, like it is washing off the dirt of this filthy world. I look back down at the body of this dirty piece of shit and smile at how I now feel so clean, covered in the contents of his skull.

There it is. Just like that. The intention. The follow through. All me. From beginning to end. This shattered mass of what used to be a face, of bone and brain, of blood and teeth, this horrible, brilliant, beautiful, destruction has cleansed and cured me. My hammer drips and I feel alive. My art is alive. My world is alive. *I am alive*. Sometimes the biggest thing in our way is ourselves.

hat a goddamn inspirational story of overcoming adversity and self-doubt. When I am getting interviewed by a nervous reporter in prison I will point to this moment as the turning point. Look to me for inspiration, I'll say. For murder or writing or painting. I'll be your goddamn idol. I'll tell them to put the pen to the paper, the paint to the canvas, or the hammer to the teeth. Start creating or destroying. I can't wait to watch the twitchy little reporter recoil in fear. I can't wait to watch the whole damn world recoil in fear.

A Word from Our Projectionist

Control. It's what everyone wants, and nobody has. It helps us get through our days, and sleep at night, to pretend we do, of course. But the little lives we build, all our routines and structures, are really no more stable than a house of cards. Just one little bump, and the whole thing has suddenly fallen down around us. And life is chock full of bumps, big and small. Your heel breaks in the middle of your work day. You get a flat tire. The barista gives you the wrong order. You get fired. Your spouse leaves you. Cancer. Covid. Natural disasters. The list goes on and on. Things *happen*. Life happens. The only real control we have is over our actions in the face of it.

So how do we reconcile the fact that most of what happens to us in our lives is completely out of our control? Do we go with the flow, and just ride the wave that is our existence, making our choices and dealing with things as they come? Or do we go the other way, tightly gripping onto whatever we can grasp, trying to control everything around us, ending up as a quivering mass of anxiety and anger? I think it's probably clear to us all that the second option is both futile and frustrating, but avoiding it is easier said than done, and I am certainly no expert.

I definitely struggle to let go. My natural inclination is to desperately try to control everything outside myself. Paramount amongst those things I try to control are the feelings of others and their perceptions of me. Perhaps you can relate? I want others to see my best side, how hard I try, how fair and kind and conscientious I can be. No one wants to be seen at their worst. When emotions run high and we've lost… control. Obviously, we cannot control what other people see and think and feel. But that irrational urge still informs our actions.

The older I get, the more I learn to let go of the things and the thoughts I cling to so tightly.

ut I do fear I started quite late, and I am not very far along that path. I keep trying to remind myself that control of anything outside myself is an illusion. It can be difficult to wrap your head around. The ego likes to think it has a say in everything. We think things to ourselves everyday like *if I don't bring an umbrella out with me, it'll surely rain.* Rationally, we know if is going to rain, it'll rain whether or not we're prepared for it. But for some reason our silly little brain meats like to pretend our actions can control even the weather.

Now, ourselves, our actions and reactions - that's a different kettle of fish. Those we can and could control, to the extent we are able. We all do it, everyday. I wake up and I want to roll over and sleep for another two hours, then spend the day eating junk and watching Netflix in bed, but instead I shut off my alarm, get dressed, and go to work. How many times in a day do we choose to be kind, or at least be silent, in the face of annoyances? How many times do we choose to be decent, to avoid aggravating a situation? We all pick our battles, and that, at its very heart, is self control.

It is far too easy, I think, to let our emotions rule us. To become reactive, fly off the handle. Maybe we keep things bottled up until something small sets us off. Then our reaction is totally out of proportion, because we've lost control. There it is again, mocking us with our inability to handle it even in small doses. Control.

Maybe we need to feel as if we have some control over the things around us, just to keep sane. Maybe the prospect of just how small and insignificant we truly are is too much for us to take. And so we imagine scenarios where we are in control, whilst letting our emotions rule over us and giving up the little bit we had in the first place.

I like to think you'll keep the idea of control in mind while you read these stories. I think all our protagonists are grappling with control, or the lack of it, in one way or another. Perhaps you'll come to look at it in a new light. Or maybe not. Que sera, sera, after all.

I

Grace lay as still as possible as the hacksaw slowly ground its way through her midsection, tearing through skin and muscle and organs. She had long grown accustomed to pain. It was remembering to look like it was all a very amusing trick that was the difficult part. Keep up the facade, don't let the mask slip. The Mysterious Massimo was now trying to saw through her spine without making it look like he was *actually* sawing through bone. That was probably difficult as well, but Grace couldn't muster up any sympathy for the man. A saw tooth caught on her spine and her smile faltered for a second as The Mysterious Massimo ground through it with a grimace of effort. Grace smiled through gritted teeth, ignoring the crunching sounds and the pangs of agony, and traveled back in time in her mind to when her poor mother had met the sick bastard.

Leanna Moore was a very pretty woman, beautiful even, but she was also a single mother, not the most respectable position for a turn of the twentieth century woman to be in. People assumed she was of loose morals. In reality, her husband had been disappointed when the son he'd dreamed of was born a daughter. He'd waited a good six months before he sneaked out of their apartment one cold January in the bleak hours of the early morning, and never returned.

Leanna was devastated, of course. Her one true love, the father of her only child, had abandoned them both in the bitter winter of the Windy City. She attempted to find work and a childminder, both hard to come by for a woman with no money and few skills. Then The Mysterious Massimo rolled into town with his wild dark hair and his charming demeanor.

His name was Teddy Fine, and he was a third rate stage magician. Mostly card tricks and sleight of hand type stuff. Nothing too complicated or original. He was nice enough to look at, not exactly handsome, but his dark hair and piercing blue eyes made him striking, at least. He had a booming voice and just enough charisma to be able to eke out a decent living on stage despite his lack of talent or outstanding tricks.

What he really wanted, the thing that would help take him to the next level, was a knock-out assistant. All the best magicians had them. A pretty little thing, all smiles and bouncing breasts. Leanna was a stunning beauty, who would blow the other assistants out of the water. Together, they would become unstoppable.

It felt like a gift from heaven when Teddy began to woo Leanna. After a series of dates, he asked Leanna work for him. They would travel the country, performing 4 evenings a week. Grace could sit in her bouncy chair backstage while Leanna and Teddy performed. The tricks themselves wouldn't take too long to learn, and they'd have plenty of time to practice. It was a big ask, but Leanna knew her prospects were slim. It was legitimate work, and she'd grown fond enough of Teddy to find the proposition favorable. Teddy was her knight in shining armor, saving her from a dull, drab and dangerous life of factory work. Why should a gal as beautiful as she was risk life and limb in some dirty old factory, he argued.

It was a story Grace had heard so many times, she almost felt the memories were her own. Within 6 months Teddy and Leanna had wed. The show was coming along quite well. The Mysterious Massimo and The Lovely Leanna were bringing in almost twice the audience that Teddy had on his own. He was able to do more complicated tricks with an assistant, and his reputation grew along the circuit. The amount of men who attended just to ogle Leanna could not be overestimated. Massimo was happy to share the sight of his beautiful assistant on stage. Letting her seduce the masses. Teddy, on the other hand, was jealous and controlling. He rarely let Leanna

ut of his sight, and the fact that they were constantly
ouring the country meant that she had no friends, and no
oots put down anywhere.

Like a caged bird, Leanna grew quietly more
epressed and lonely as the years rolled by. It wasn't long
efore the only place she smiled was onstage. She loved
e attention she got from the audience, and only truly felt
ive under their adoring gaze.

Grace caused havoc by running around backstage
nd getting under everyone's feet. There was a wildness
 her that sparked joy in Leanna and utter contempt in
Mr." Teddy. He shouted and threatened, but Grace paid
m no mind. There was something in her that spurred her
, despite his obvious and vocal disapproval. She felt
fe under the watchful eyes of her mother, and let her
ildness run free.

Grace vividly remembered the day Teddy found
t she was magic. She was seven, a remarkably healthy
ild who never seemed to fall ill, chock full of energy
d nerve. When the other performer's children all got
e croup, she was still running around, full of vigor.
ace never caught the pox, or the measles. These
ildhood illnesses would quickly spread throughout the
eater community, but Grace would always be underfoot,
nk cheeked and sweaty from running around backstage.

She grew bored watching as her mother and Mr.
ddy practiced some tedious new trick with her mother
 a box, disappearing. It was obvious to Grace that there
ere two doors, and her mother was simply sneaking out
e back. Grace climbed the purchase line high above
e stage. She hung there swinging her legs and laughing
til she looked down and saw the fear in her mother's
es. Then she lost her grip.

Grace tumbled down. She reached out for the line,
t her fingers brushed it and caught nothing but air. Then
ere was a thud and a sickening crack and dull pain and
rkness.

When she came to, her mother's tear streaked face
s above her, eyes wide with shock and joy. Behind her,
. Teddy's eyes were lit with an emotion she'd never
en in them before. His smile was crooked and full of
alice. But there was no pain, and Grace jumped up,
nning off as though nothing had happened at all.

Leanna had told her that she'd landed on
ne costumes, and they'd broken her fall, but Grace
membered nothing but the cold hard wood of the stage
neath her. As the years passed she came to suspect
t she had been *very* badly injured in the fall, at least
tially. The truth was, Grace knew that the cuts and

scrapes she got in her normal play disappeared within a
few seconds, and she rarely ever felt them. She'd seen it
countless times. Once her mother had pulled out a splinter
and they'd both watch as the tiny hole had closed up
before their eyes in an instant. Her mother had stared but
said nothing. Grace followed her lead and never spoke of
it either.

From that day on, Mr. Teddy took more interest
in Grace. What she did, where she went, who she spoke
to. He hovered in the doorway, watching when Leanna
taught Grace to read and to add and subtract. He noted
what sort of treats she liked and brought her candied
apples and tarts when she managed to stay out of trouble.
Which became more and more often as Leanna's health
deteriorated. As the weeks passed after Grace's fall,
Leanna became weaker, and thinner. She picked up a
cough that stuck around and became more and more
pronounced. Grace believed the scare of her fall had
made her mother ill. So she sat quietly by her bed, no
more running or climbing, hoping her acts of contrition
would somehow make Leanna well again. It didn't.

Grace smiled and winked at the audience as
Teddy pulled two metal sheets out and slid them into
the two halves of the box. Then he spun the boxes
around separately, showing off his handiwork. He then
pushed the halves back together, and quickly pulled
the metal plates back out as he covered the box with a
sheet, leaving only Grace's head and feet visible to the
audience. Most magicians would show that their assistant
was whole at this point, but not the Mysterious Massimo.
He walked out in front of Grace and began doing sleight
of hand and card tricks. Grace's flesh took a minute to
fully heal, and it wouldn't do to let the audience *see* that
healing. It would ruin the whole trick and cause a riot.

Grace's mind wandered as Teddy performed the
absolute oldest trick in the book, the ball and cups trick.
She thought back to the day he'd heard about the Selbit
sawing. She was sixteen and had just taken over from the
string of girls who had replaced her mother. Finally old
enough and attractive enough with her mother's coloring,
Mr. Teddy insisted she start earning her keep. Nevermind
all the cooking and cleaning she did, she was to follow in
her mother's footsteps. Grace tried not to think too deeply
about everything that would entail.

Mr. Teddy had gotten a costume made for her,
and studied her intently in it. It had green and white
stripes with rhinestones all over the bodice. The bottom
was overlaid with a green fringe. It brought out her eyes,
which were shining deep watery pools, just like Leanna's
had been. Her strawberry blonde hair rolled down her

shoulders in soft waves. She was pretty enough, with good bones and an upturned nose, but not the great classic beauty her mother had been in her youth. *She'll do*, Teddy thought. He knew he had something special on his hands, he just had to figure out how to utilize her.

She was trying on her new costume when Mr. Teddy picked up the newspaper and read about P.T. Selbit sawing a woman in half the week before on stage in London. His eyes glazed over in a way that Grace knew could only mean trouble. It would be ages before he attempted to turn his sudden brain storm into a reality. He would start a bit smaller and see what he could do.

To start off with, Mr. Teddy trained her to hold his props and hand them over without exposing any secrets. Grace picked things up quickly enough, and by the end of the week he'd christened her *The Lovely Galinda*, and debuted her on stage.

The audience seemed drawn to her, sucked in by her pretty eyes and youthful good looks. They would eventually come to worship her like her mother. Soon, Teddy and Grace's practice sessions would turn to darker tricks.

They attempted the Indian basket trick, which was an old one, but Teddy had thought of an amazing twist. *Show* the audience the inside of the basket. It would, of course, look like a normal basket instead of a trick one. That was because it would indeed be a normal basket. Grace would climb in, and with the audience thinking there was nowhere for her to hide, he would thrust the swords through. He would pull them back out , and Grace would emerge from the basket whole.

It was a lovely idea, but of course, he hadn't thought things through. Grace tended to shout every time he thrust a sword through her. That was problem one. Now, Grace did not feel much in the way of pain - when she cut herself or banged a knee, she barely felt a tickle. But she did feel pain if she was pushed far enough. Multiple swords stuck willy-nilly, inches deep in her body was, indeed, far enough. Teddy's solution was for her to get used to the feeling. For hours, he would stick the swords in and pull them back out, allowing her a few minutes to heal up before starting the process all over again. She hated him for it, but he was partially correct in his assumption. She didn't so much grow used to the pain, as much as she grew good at hiding it. Teddy didn't really care if she was in complete agony, as long as she could act like she didn't feel anything at all.

There was, of course, blood on the swords when he pulled them out. He found if he pulled them out slowly and leaned into the basket with the blade, the blood left over was minimal, and could be played off as fake blood for effect.

The blood left on Grace was a different problem altogether. Teddy solved this by lining the domed lid of the basket with a damp towel. Once the swords were removed, Grace would slip the towel out and wipe off her quickly closing wounds. She could then stuff the towel back into the lid. The audience were, of course, sure the trick was in the basket, not the lid. They practiced the trick with this method for a fortnight before Teddy finally decided it was time to test it out on stage.

Grace fidgeted backstage. If anyone realized she was a freak, they would take her away. She'd be locked in some lab and tested on for the rest of her life. Mr. Teddy told her this daily. How that would be different from what they'd been doing for the past few weeks, she wasn't sure. But the idea of being locked in a lab forever scared her nonetheless.

The trick went off without a hitch. Grace huddled quietly in the basket while the Mysterious Massimo stabbed swords into her. One went straight through her forearm. Another pierced just behind her ribs. The third embedded in the meat of her thigh. Then he pulled the swords out and started the next trick. About halfway through some guess-the-card trick, The Lovely Galinda would jump from the basket, completely unharmed. The audience would gasp, then laugh as the Mysterious Massimo feigned surprise and annoyance at his card trick being disrupted. Then he'd pull the card from Galinda's costume with a flourish, and the audience would erupt into cheers and whistles.

Grace wiggled around in the box. She felt whole and solid, and gave a tiny little cough that no one but The Mysterious Massimo could hear. The illusionist wrapped up his trick and pushed Grace and her box forward.

"Here we have the Lovely Galinda, all rested up after being cut thoroughly down the middle and put back together again." With this, The Mysterious Massimo dropped the side panel and opened the top of both halves of the box. As she slid out smiling, the Mysterious Massimo bowed at her, and passed her a fan of giant green feathers, behind which she hid her damp towel. The audience gasped and then cheered and clapped, and Grace beamed at them, basking in their adoration. If performing with the Mysterious Massimo was torture, then the appreciation of the audience was the release of bindings and the relief of unconsciousness all rolled into one.

Teddy and Grace bowed and waved, and stepped off stage.

"You were distracted tonight, and it showed. Get
urself together, girl."

Grace wilted silently beneath Mr. Teddy's glare.
e *was* distracted. It was part of how she coped with
 pain she could still feel. She lost herself to memories,
eping one tentative toe in reality just enough to know
en to smile and wink, and react to the audience.
e would have to be more careful at tomorrow's
rformance. The last thing she needed was Mr. Teddy's
ath. There was only one show left this week, and then
efully she'd get a day or two of peace.

Grace headed off to take a hot bath and unwind.
e perfumed the bath with Leanna's favorite scent
 sunk into the steaming water with a sigh. The tiny
om was filled with the scent of lemons, bergamot, and
mine. The whole experience felt like a warm hug from
 mother. Grace let the water swallow her head to toe,
 lay there for a moment just letting reality go. When
 could hold her breath no longer, she emerged from
 tub, skin glowing pink from the heat, and toweled
self off. She slipped into her silken night clothes and
ried herself off to bed. Finally it was time for blissful
.

It was three in the morning when her door
aked open. Light from the hallway fell onto her face
 the stink of charcoal, sickly sweet corn and ethanol
m cheap whiskey roused her. Mr. Teddy stood in the
orway, in his undershirt, trousers, and suspenders
king down on her with dark eyes that didn't seem able
ocus.

"You were the only good thing in my life, Lee."
"Mr. Teddy, it's really late," Grace panicked at the
 of his pet name for Leanna.
"Don't fucking call me that!" Teddy spat,
owing the empty bottle at the far wall. Grace flinched
he broken bottle rained glass all over the floor.

Teddy stumbled towards the bed, tearing at his
penders. He stood above Grace swaying erratically.

"You were always too good for me, and you knew
idn't ya, Lee?"

Grace sat frozen in her bed. She couldn't seem to
e herself to move, even though she knew what came
t. Teddy undid his trousers and let them drop to the
r.

"You never let me forget it, either."
Then he was on top of her, all hot stinking breath
 grasping, calloused fingers tearing away her silk
amas. Grace's body would not obey her, so she lay
e whimpering while Teddy tore off her clothes and
ped inside of her. He thrust into her fast and clumsy,

hissing vile names in her ear.

"*Cunt. Whore. Bitch*," he spluttered, the sour
whiskey smell of his breath invading her nostrils. His
fingers dug into her wrists as he held her down. She
didn't fight, she just sobbed as he violated her body in yet
another way, hating herself for her inability to fight back.
When he finally ejaculated, his back arched and an angry
growl escaped him. Teddy immediately passed out on top
of her. Grace lay there letting the tears trickle down her
face.

Finally regaining control of her body, Grace
rolled Teddy onto his back and slipped out of the bed.
She grabbed her day clothes and ran to the bathroom,
locking herself inside. She ran the hot water and soaked
a rag, then wiped herself with it. The tears came hot and
fast. He'd never been like a father to Grace, but he'd kept
her when her mother died. He'd bought her clothes and
fed her and, as painful as it was, made her part of a very
successful act. Even more successful than he'd been with
her mother. Somehow she'd convinced herself that he
cared for her, at least a bit.

Now she knew how utterly and truly alone she
really was.

The act was becoming increasingly popular. They were
packing houses that months before were only half full.
Teddy began to think up variations on the most violent
tricks. The audience was taken in more, the more
harrowing the tricks seemed. He designed new boxes, and
sawed off Grace's limbs. It was a fresh new torture for
Grace, but she learned something quite interesting.

One night, on stage, after The Mysterious
Massimo had cut through her arms and pulled the boxes
apart, Grace *waved* to the audience. A small titter went
up from those who'd noticed, but Teddy was busy setting
up the next trick and didn't react. Up until this point,
she'd never tried to move a disconnected limb. Now that
she knew she could do it, she decided to keep it secret
from Teddy. Finally she had something of her own that he
couldn't use against her.

On the rare occasion Grace had some time to

herself, she'd go and watch the other performances at the theaters. She loved the Vaudeville shows, and would often sit and watch act after act. Acrobats, comedians, jugglers, singers, dancers, trained animals, even the competition, other magicians. Grace enjoyed the escape from her own life for a few hours.

Unlike Leanna, who was never allowed the freedom to leave Teddy's side, Grace was welcome to do what she willed with her free time. In fact, it seemed as though her presence was not wanted, outside of her chores and dry runs of their performance. Teddy seemed ill at ease whenever Grace was around, scowling and muttering to himself. It seemed better to avoid him as much as possible.

Sometimes Teddy would follow her to the shows, most frequently when the other illusionists were performing, sitting back far enough where Grace didn't know he was there. He'd watch the light-hearted tricks with shoelaces, balloons and scarves all played to the upbeat tune of a piano and scoff. There was no drama, no danger. To Teddy it looked like a mockery of the very serious performance art he was trying to achieve. After a few trips, he left Grace to it. He had no interest in silly performances.

Grace, for her part, memorized the songs and dance steps. She would sneak out onto the stage when Teddy was out drinking himself stupid, and sing and dance to her heart's content. One night, she had an audience. When Grace reached the end of a song, he stood up in the dark and gave her a standing ovation. Grace ran from the stage, but he followed her out into the dark alley behind the theater.

"I'm really sorry, I didn't mean to scare you. I loved your singing."

Grace stood with her back to him, tears lining her face.

"Look, it's late. I can't leave you out here alone. It's not safe outside. Please come back in." He held a hand out to her. "My name is Jimmy. Jimmy Vance. I'm a juggler. I'm not actually all that good yet. I'm still in training, you see? I'm really awfully sorry."

Grace looked at him. He was young, maybe 17. He was of wiry build and just a bit taller than Grace. He had curly hair and his skin was golden brown. His eyes looked honest and Grace decided then to forgive him. She took his hand and he led her back indoors.

"I didn't mean anything. I was just sitting out here in the dark, trying to imagine myself on stage when you came out and started singing. You've got a really sweet voice, anyway. I didn't want to interrupt. What's your name? Let's be friends."

"I'm Grace. Grace Moore. I'm a magician's assistant. I thought I was alone. I'd never have done tha in front of anyone."

"You should though! I think you're awfully talented, Grace. You could be a chorus line girl, no fooling." Jimmy looked at the floor then looked back up at Grace. "Do you come out here a lot at night? I do. I can't sleep and I come out here and sit in the stands and try to imagine myself as a real performer."

Grace nodded. "I come out here and sing whenever my stepfather is off drinking. It's easy to get away and I don't really wanna be there when he comes home."

Jimmy nodded but had enough tact not to pry. He slapped his knee. "Hey, I've got an idea. We can be each other's audience! No one else needs to know. We can get practice performing and get ourselves used to an audience. Well, I suppose you already *are* used to one. But not for your singing. We can just meet up and perform for each other and have a nice chat afterwards. What do ya say, Gracie?"

Jimmy looked at her with big, pleading brown eyes. He seemed so sweet and earnest that she couldn't help but agree.

"Okay, Jimmy. I'll come here when I can, and w can perform for each other."

Jimmy punched the air joyfully. "Hot dog! I'm going to practice and be really good for you, Grace, I promise."

Grace blushed at his excitement. "I really ough get back now, Jimmy. See ya soon!" She favored him with a smile and ran off toward the side exit that border her and Teddy's rooms at the hotel next door. She snuc into her room, closing the door as quietly as possible. S put an ear to the wall and could hear a distinct snoring from next door. Teddy must have passed out in his cups again. Grace sighed with relief and changed into her ni clothes. Tomorrow they would perform, so she needed rest up. They were adding a newly improved Firewalk the routine. Grace would be expected to set it all up, an it involved a metal frame, bags of sand and a lot of coa

When Grace curled up under her covers, it was Jimmy's face that appeared to her unbidden. His gentle smile and his warm, kind eyes. He held out his hand to her. Grace slept peacefully.

It was thirty minutes until they were due on stage. Grace was there, in costume, emptying the sandbags into the low metal frame. Once the bags were empty she used a rake to smooth it all down evenly. Then she started shoveling a thin layer of coal on top. Once the coal was evenly distributed, Grace ran back to the dressing room to freshen up her makeup. If she didn't look perfect, she was sure to hear about it.

Grace touched up her rouge and kohl and sprayed herself with the nearest bottle of perfume she found. She straightened up her hair then headed back out to the stage. It was time to put on a big toothy grin and go through the motions.

The spotlight shone down on the Mysterious Massimo. With a great flourish of his hand, he lit the coals, starting at the back of the stage and slowly walking towards the audience, lighting all the coal along the way. When he got to the end, he shut his pocket lighter with another flourish. The Mysterious Massimo then smiled at the audience. When he spoke, his voice boomed out across the theater.

"I am the Mysterious Massimo. Tonight you will witness feats beyond your imagination. I would like to introduce to you, my delightful assistant," here he paused and with a sweeping gesture of his arm, continued, "The lovely Galinda!"

At this a spotlight hit Grace, who smiled, gestured to her bare feet, then stepped out onto the red hot, freshly lit coals. She paused for a beat, then very slowly walked towards the audience. She placed each foot carefully so as not to rush the effect, but tried to move each foot before the coals could sear into her flesh too deeply. When she reached the front of the stage, she curtsied, then turned and walked back the way she had come, through the coals, slowly. Then she headed backstage and stuck her feet in a bucket of cool water to help speed up the healing process.

"My friends, the wonders you will see tonight will change your understanding of the very basics of the natural world. But do not fear! We shall guide you through this labyrinth of the strange and impossible. Trust in the Mysterious Massimo, and the Lovely Galinda!" As he finished his speech, The lovely Galida appeared back on stage. She sat in a chair and put on her heels, making sure the audience got a good glimpse of the bottoms of her pristine feet. Then she brought Massimo his next prop and stood to the side, gesturing and smiling, handing him props and other assistant jobs until it was time to stick her arms into boxes he had specially made.

There were two of them, and they sat upon a frame. Grace stood between them with her arms inside. They joined into halves just below her elbows. She smiled through gritted teeth as the Mysterious Massimo sawed through first one arm and then the other. Grace made a shocked face as he swung the frames outward, clearly separating the bottom half of her arms from the top.

"See how my lovely assistant feels no pain whatsoever!" Massimo gestured towards Grace with a sweep of his arm, then pushed the boxes back into place. He began shuffling his cards, and The lovely Galinda gave the audience a thumbs up with a wink.

No one knew exactly how the tricks worked, but they ate it up. The crowd loved the smiling, winking Galinda and the debonair gentleman who pretended to dismember her. It was all ever so exciting. Grace looked out into the audience at the adoring faces and saw one she wasn't expecting. Jimmy stood amongst the audience, clapping politely but looking thoughtful and concerned. Grace knew he would have questions that she wasn't sure she could answer.

Teddy was in a fine mood after their performance. "Much better tonight, Grace. Maybe we'll make something out of you after all." He headed off for the bar down the street, where he knew he'd be bought drinks by the adoring audience, especially the men who wanted to know more about the Lovely Galinda.

Grace went back to the room and put on her nicest dress, a bit out of date, long and floaty, but pretty even though not the latest fashion. She made herself a sandwich for supper, then fixed her rouge and headed back to the stage. Jimmy was waiting for her with a bag full of balls. Grace settled into a front row seat and smiled at him in encouragement.

Jimmy threw one, two, three balls in the air. After a couple passes he threw a fourth. Then a fifth. He kept them up for a few turns, then he threw one in a different pattern while he kept the others up. Then two, three, four, then finally he caught all five and bowed deeply. Grace stood up and erupted with applause.

"I thought you said you weren't very good!" Grace said, climbing up onto the stage.

"I'm not!" Jimmy protested, "That's very basic stuff right there. I'm only just starting out, really." Jimmy stared at his shoes as though he'd not seen them before. "Did you like it, then?"

"It was wonderful, Jimmy! I think *you're* wonderful." Grace stopped for a second, then quickly kissed Jimmy's cheek. She cast her gaze to the floorboards.

"Look at us," Jimmy said, laughing. "Can't even look each other in the eyes." He then stopped, expression serious. "Gracie, when you do those tricks, you're smiling but you don't look happy. Does it–does it hurt you, any of that?" Jimmy searched her eyes, looking for answers.

"It's a bit of a long story, Jimmy. I would really like to tell you everything. Maybe I will, sometime. But not tonight. Tonight, can we just have fun?" Grace grabbed his hand and squeezed it twice, in a pleading gesture.

"Anything for you, Gracie Moore. Anything you say."

Jimmy's troupe played two weeks at the same theater as The Mysterious Massimo before they had to move on. Grace and Jimmy hugged tightly, and promised to keep an eye out for each other's shows. They would meet up again clandestinely as soon as they could.

Teddy and Grace spent that evening and part of the next day traveling by bus to the next destination. Cleveland Ohio was next up on their itinerary. The cities they visited all seemed pretty much the same to Grace. She never got to explore them beyond the walk from the hotel to the theater. Teddy didn't exactly stop her from going out, but he made his feelings on everything she did loudly and clearly plain. It wasn't really worth the hassle to go out and do anything Teddy hadn't explicitly ordered her to do, so she rarely did.

When Teddy went out, Grace would sing all the songs she knew from the other shows. Today she was dancing around her room singing one such song.

"They say I'm crazy, got no sense, but I don't care. They may or may not mean offense, but I don't care." Grace spun around the room, singing with her eyes closed. "You see I'm sort of independent, clever…" Grace stopped spinning and opened her eyes at the sound of the latch.

There stood Teddy staring at her. There was a moment of shocked silence between the two of them, then Teddy began to laugh. He dropped the newspaper he was holding and bent at the waist, holding his stomach as he let out a raucous guffaw. Grace's face turned beet red as rage tears stung at her eyes. This made Teddy laugh even harder.

"Do you think you're any good, Grace? Gonna give up magic and become a singer, are ya?" Teddy slapped his knee and laughed at the ridiculousness of it all. Grace pushed past him and ran out into the hall, down the stairs and out through the lobby into the street. His

laughter followed on her heels. She kept running.

Grace found herself at the only place she knew how to get to, the theater. She took herself in a side entrance and hid backstage with all the props and scenery. She sobbed quietly, ashamed of herself and how Teddy made her feel. Why should she feel bad? Why *shouldn't* she sing and dance? Who was Teddy to make her feel this way? Far from the first time, she wished her mother had never met him. Better she'd grown up destitute than owing anything to this horrible man.

Her thoughts turned to Jimmy. How she wished she had her friend here now. He always made her feel safe and important, somehow. Grace wondered when she'd see him again.

When Grace finally returned to her rooms, Teddy was nowhere to be found. Relieved at his absence, Grace filled the bath with steaming water, and climbed in for a nice, cleansing cry. Grace wondered idly if this is the life Leanna would have wanted for her. Slave to the whims of her mother's lover. *Oh mother, what do I do?*

Grace pictured her mother sitting beside the tub with a sponge, wiping her forehead softly. Leanna would have hummed her a soothing tune, and told her that she had to do what made her happy. That's what she would have wanted. Grace decided that she must find a way to enjoy her life, whatever that took. She had to do this for the memory of her mother.

The weeks passed by like the trickling of molasses. Teddy switched up the act every so often, so the audience didn't know which gruesome tricks will be shown on any given night. Will they see a pretty girl sawed in half, or simply dismembered? Will she be run through with swords, or walk through burning coals? Teddy was desperate to find new and interesting ways to use Grace's ability to amaze and astound the audience, but he was running out of ideas.

Grace, for her part, kept checking the line up to see who was on the bill, hoping beyond hope that Jimmy Vance would be playing the same theater as them. She'd watch all the performances whenever she could. She'd quietly sing along from her seat, but she would never take the chance of singing out loud in her rooms again. It was a humiliation she just couldn't bring herself to face once more.

Grace wandered the empty theater at night, after all the performers had packed up and gone back to their rooms. It was so lonely these days. She was too old to make friends with the children, and too shy to stand

ound chatting with the real performers. If she went back
her rooms, she might run into drunken Teddy, her least
vorite version of the man.

Finally, after two and a half months of lousy
ck, there they were, on the bill. The Vivacious Vance
mily. Grace was overjoyed to finally get to see Jimmy
ain. She wasn't even performing until tomorrow, so she
uld go watch his family's act and everything. Grace
t on an ankle grazing dress and a spot or two of rouge.
ting herself as dolled up as she could manage without
using Teddy's suspicions, and ran down to the theater
watch the show. The songs were new and upbeat. The
medians were brash and bold. Jimmy performed with
family, juggling steadily in the background while they
performed various feats around him. Grace enjoyed
ery minute and clapped and whooped along with the
dience the whole way through, thinking it was the best
formance she'd seen in ages.

When it was all over, Grace moved up towards
front row and sat quietly waiting as the performers
hered their things and trickled out in twos and threes.
entually, only Grace and Jimmy were left in the entire
ater. She ran up to the stage and stopped just in front
im. Jimmy opened his arms wide and Grace threw
self into them.

"I've really missed you, Jimmy!" Grace
laimed. The tears came unbidden.

"Oh, Gracie, no. Don't cry! I've missed you too."
my nuzzled into her hair just the slightest bit. It was
t and scented like strawberries. "Why are you so sad?"

Suddenly, Grace was telling him everything. Her
ther, her secret, the way Teddy's tricks worked. The
y he'd *laughed* when he found her singing. The awful
r that she would be stuck here, doing this, for the rest
her life. Grace didn't know how long she talked, but
was all cried out by the time she was done.

Jimmy held her by the shoulders and got down on
knees to look up at her. "I promise you, Grace, this
l not be forever. We will find you a way out of this. I
l help you however I can."

Grace sniffled and wiped at her eyes. "You
mise, Jimmy?"

Jimmy put his hand over his heart, "I swear it to
, Gracie Moore. Now will you sing me a tune?"

Grace nodded and prepared herself as Jimmy
mbed back down into the seats below. Once he was
led in he gave her a nod and a wink, and Gracie began

"My heart is sad and I'm all alone, my man treats
mean…"

When she'd finished, Jimmy gave her a standing

ovation, whooping and clapping til his hands hurt. Then
he walked her out to the front of her hotel, keeping a
watchful eye on her. Grace gave him a quick peck on
the cheek, then ran upstairs before he could react. Up
on the third floor, there was a rustle of the curtains in
the window of Teddy's room, looking down on the hotel
entrance.

Grace went up to her room giggling, her cheeks
hot and pink all giddy from everything that she'd done.
Yes she'd given Jimmy a kiss, sure, but more importantly,
she'd shared her secret, *and he didn't run screaming.*
Grace took a hat pin and scratched her arm, not deeply,
but enough to draw blood. Jimmy stared in shock as the
cut closed itself up in seconds. Grace stared intently at
Jimmy, waiting for the inevitable rejection, but it never
came.

"Gracie," he'd said, "you're magic! Like actual,
real life magic."

Grace sighed out a deep breath she didn't even
realize she'd held in. Tears welled up in her eyes and she
wrung her hands.

"You mean it, Jimmy? You're not afraid of me?"

"How could I be afraid of you, Gracie the magic
girl? You're the best girl I've ever met."

Grace kicked off her shoes and rubbed her feet.
She thought about what she'd have to eat, as she'd
skipped dinner, when the door to her room banged open.
There stood Teddy, face red and angry, without a whiff of
booze about him.

"Just who *exactly* was that boy I saw you with,
Grace?" Teddy huffed, face red and angry.

"He's just a friend I made, Teddy. What's wrong?"
Grace's heart hammered in her throat. She began to
sweat. She'd never seen Teddy this angry before.

"He's just a friend I made," Teddy mocked her.
"Who told you you could have boyfriends, Grace? What
have you told him? *What does he know?"*

"I haven't told him anything, Teddy, I swear! I
would never tell anyone any of our secrets." Grace began
crying. She didn't know what he was going to do next,
but she knew it wouldn't be anything good.

What Teddy did next was pick up a heavy carved
glass ashtray, and swing it directly at Grace's face. She
turned away at the last second, and the ashtray connected
with the side of her skull. There was a cracking noise in
the midst of the heavy thunk of contact. Blood poured
from the wound the ashtray had created. Teddy swung
it again, widening the now sizable hole. Broken shards
of skull and dripping brain matter coated the edge of
the glass. Grace fell to the floor, and Teddy was on

her immediately. He slapped her across the face then choked her until the room swam in her vision. A long line of spittle hung from his mouth dangling just above her forehead. She watched it swing back and forth, wondering if this was how she died.

Grace curled up like a pill bug as Teddy went on beating her. He slammed her head on the floor. Bones cracked and blood splattered, but these things fixed themselves so quickly that by the time Teddy had tired himself out, one could barely tell he'd touched her at all. Grace moaned quietly as her body knit itself back together.

"You disgust me, you filthy whore! Your mother would be so ashamed of you, galavanting with some boy that you barely even know. I should leave you out on the street, where you belong. Sell yourself to anyone with a penny!" With that, Teddy straightened his clothes and stalked off out of Grace's rooms, slamming the door behind him.

Grace dragged herself up and over to the bath. She ran the water as she let out great heaving sobs. How could things go so wrong so quickly? She climbed into the steaming water and washed herself gently, tired of the way they both treated her body like a thing that didn't matter, just because it would right itself. Her body was *her,* and she cared what happened to it. Why was she letting this man treat her this way?

Because you have nowhere else to go and no one else to care for you, Grace answered herself. But Teddy didn't care for her. He cared for his standing as The Mysterious Massimo. He cared about applause, and how many seats were sold. He cared about the audience wondering *how*? But Grace? Grace was just a tool. A means to an end. Grace wondered if Leanna had meant anything more to him than she did. Deep down, she doubted it.

There was an upside to all of this. Teddy could not break her spirit, and he'd proven pretty incapable of hurting her body in any meaningful way. Her ability was too quick, she healed up by the time he was readying himself for the next strike. She supposed he could find a way to kill her, if he really thought about it. But he was unlikely to manage it in a fit of anger.

Grace would have to be extremely careful meeting up with Jimmy from now on, though. She had been careful not to give Teddy any information about who Jimmy was, but he wouldn't be hard to track down for the next week, if Teddy wanted to. Grace decided to make sure she got to Jimmy first and let him know that he might be in danger from Teddy. She would never forgive

herself if her friendship caused him any harm. He was a nice boy who only wanted to help her. He certainly didn' deserve whatever Teddy might have in store for him.

Grace Moore snuck backstage during the next day's show. She waved Jimmy down, and he followed her into a dressing room. Only after she assured herself the weren't followed by scanning the hallway did she close the door.

"What's with all the cloak and dagger, Gracie?"

"Oh Jimmy, it was terrible!" Grace fell into Jimmy's arms. "He saw us outside the hotel. He called a whore and he tried to beat me to death. Bashed in my head and everything." At this Jimmy pushed Grace bac his own face stoney and tight. Grace grabbed his arms and forced him to look her in the eyes. "Don't even thi about it, Jimmy. He's a monster. You've gotta lay low. would never forgive myself if he hurt you."

Jimmy scoffed at this. "I'm not afraid of some heel who beats up girls."

"I'm telling ya Jimmy, don't antagonize him. Better he doesn't know what's coming until I'm alread gone."

"Okay, Gracie, whatever you say. But one word from you and I'll beat him senseless."

That night's performance proved a harsh one for Grace. She was sawed in half, put in the basket, and made to walk the burning coals all in one evening. The audience, all except for Jimmy, were mesmerized. Grac grit her teeth and smiled beatifically at them, her head filled with dreams of escape and a life filled with pleas rather than pain, love rather than use and control.

Teddy, for his part, did every act of violence wi slow, deliberate care. He took real pleasure in sawing a her midsection and sliding the swords in. He smiled an winked at the audience, his rage bubbling beneath the surface. He gloried in the pain and power he held over little Grace Moore.

Grace took everything he gave, and more. She took all the pain, all the rage, all the hatred and she transmuted it into the will to go on, to find her way out this prison, to find herself a life of happiness. Grace curtsied and bowed, smiled and nodded, but more importantly, she endured. And the spark of the feisty little girl who climbed the purchase line and didn't care *what* Teddy thought reignited. She was herself again.

Jimmy, for his part, came up with plans. First he would buy Grace a wig, her hair was like a beacon, maybe something in a nice mousey brown to blend in with everyone else. Then they'd sneak her onto his family's bus right before their performance. She would hide in the closet. When his family were done performing, they'd pack up onto the bus and head straight out. Once they were safely out of town, Jimmy would tell them all about how Teddy treated Grace, leaving out the healing bit. His family were good people, they'd help him hide her. Then they'd figure out a way for her to get a job traveling with them. All Grace had to do was get out of Teddy's sight long enough to sneak on the bus.

Jimmy saved up his pennies to try to finance Grace's escape, but his wages were scant and money was tight. He wasn't entirely sure he'd be able to come up with enough money for the wig, let alone enough money to feed Grace until she could figure out a job.

Teddy followed Grace relentlessly after he learned of Jimmy's existence. The only way Grace was able to meet Jimmy at all was by getting lost in the crowd and sneaking backstage as the theater started to empty. Teddy's habit of watching from the back made it impossible for him to keep eyes on her once the audience stood up and began to move.

As long as she was quick about their clandestine meetings, Teddy couldn't prove she'd done anything. Luckily, the acts were filled with young men, any number of which might pass for Jimmy on that night that Teddy had witnessed Grace jumping up to kiss a man in a hat and long coat. All he knew was that Jimmy was taller than Grace, and fairly fit.

When Grace did dally too long with Jimmy, there was hell to pay. One particular night, Teddy waited in her rooms in a vest and trousers beside the door. When Grace came in, he grabbed her and shoved a sock in her mouth. Then he removed his belt, and whipped her with the metal tipped end until his arms got tired.

Grace lay there looking for the bruises and cuts that had already healed themselves. What Teddy didn't know, couldn't know, was exactly how much faster Grace was healing. It seemed like the more he beat her, the faster her skin knit itself back together. What had taken minutes to heal before, took about thirty seconds now. She was becoming stronger, and that was another secret

she would never tell him. When the time came, and it would come soon, she knew, these secrets would be her weapon.

Teddy became even more sadistic. First he built new boxes, he premiered them one night without warning Grace. He strapped in her legs and arms so she was positioned like a starfish, then he gleefully cut off each limb at the elbow or knee. The boxes and Grace's body were propped up on a spinning platform. He spun her around so the audience could get a good look at all her limbs separated from their roots. The audience gasped and recoiled. Grace tried to hide the horror and abject fear from showing on her face. Teddy grinned maniacally at the audience.

"The Lovely Limbless Girl, just for you, dear audience!" he announced with a flourish of his arm.

The audience went wild with a standing ovation as Teddy clicked the boxes back together, looking Grace dead in the eye with each *click*. Grace's body shook. *What if he'd left her like that?* It didn't bear thinking about. Grace looked out at the audience, taking in their hungry, wild eyes as they beat their hands together. She hated them almost as much as she hated Teddy at that moment.

Jimmy's troupe was leaving that night, but Teddy didn't take his eyes off Grace for a second. There was no sneaking off to hide on a bus. There was only Teddy, standing over her as she polished his swords and packed up their belongings. She rushed through the work as quickly as she could, making it through just in time to finally sneak off and say goodbye to Jimmy.

"Listen Gracie, the next time we meet, I *will* take you away from all this, I promise you." Jimmy felt useless as he held her close. "I swear, I'll have everything ready."

Grace pulled away and looked him in the eyes. "I know you will." Then she kissed him, full on the mouth. In Jimmy's mind, her strawberries and cream tasting kiss was a promise, but in Grace's it was a last goodbye. She couldn't wait months for her freedom. She would have to save herself. Whatever happened next, it would be on Grace's terms.

Grace left Jimmy and the rest of the Vances packing up to leave. Her head was filled with dark thoughts, and she decided to walk around the theater district before settling back at her hotel. She no longer feared the night, or what a strange man might do to her. All her terrors lived in the form of a man who was quietly trailing her the entire evening, without her knowledge, his anger building to a boiling point that even frightened him, a little.

The dark streets and the light rain did little to soothe her mind. How was she ever going to sneak away from Teddy? She had nothing and no one to turn to now that Jimmy's family were safely ensconced on their bus, headed for the next town. Grace ruminated the whole walk back to the hotel. It wasn't until she turned the key in her door that she felt his presence behind her.

Teddy pushed her into the room and locked the door behind him.

"Had a fun night with your boyfriend, filthy whore? Had a nice kiss goodbye?"

Grace didn't answer. There was no point, Teddy wasn't really speaking to her. She'd long come to realize he didn't think of her as a person at all.

"You think you're fooling me? You think you're fooling *anyone*? I know what you are, Grace." Teddy smacked her across the face. She barely felt the blow, but was swamped with the humiliation it was meant to convey. Teddy grabbed her, spun her around, and tore at her clothes, pushing them out of his way as he slammed her face up against the wall. His fingers dug into her arms as he penetrated her over and over.

"You're dirt. A freak. You are *nothing and no one*. Nobody loves you. Nobody cares. Yet you still think you're better than me. JUST. LIKE. YOUR. MOTHER." He grabbed her by the hair, spinning her around to face him. He spat at her, then pushed her onto the bed. Teddy continued to thrust into her, staring directly into her eyes, mocking her.

"Oh *Gracie*, where is your boyfriend now? Is he coming to save you?" Grace began to sob. Teddy licked at her tears as he continued to spear her. Then he laughed. His laughter echoed through the room. Grace left her body then. She floated off into happier memories and didn't come back until he was done, standing over her and buttoning up his trousers.

"You disgust me, Grace."

Then he walked off out of her room, and Grace Moore knew that she was going to murder Teddy Fine.

It started with Grace sneaking into Teddy's room when he was out drinking. She found where he hid his money, in a dirty old sock at the back of a drawer, and she'd skim a bit. A nickel here, a few pennies there. She was going to need coin to run. She was going to need hair dye and a bus ticket and money for food. She didn't know how much anything really cost out there, but the show was successful, and Teddy never paid her a penny, so there was enough lying around to dip into without anyone taking notice.

Her next step was to start walking. Out of the theater district, into the city. She'd keep track of each turn and how many blocks she walked. She was going to need to make a fast escape, and being scared and lost were not options she could afford. She sketched out a crude map. She would do it for this town, and the next one… as many as she needed to until it was time to put her plan into action.

Grace became single-minded in her spare time, no longer worrying about whether or not Jimmy was in town, or how she could find happiness. Her path had become clear. *Nothing* mattered more than her freedom. Happiness could not exist, let alone a relationship with Jimmy or anyone else, without that freedom. She was beginning to feel as if her whole world was balanced on the edge of a knife. More than that, as if multiple worlds, multiple lifetimes were held in the balance. Grace felt as if everything happening was somehow bigger than her in a way she just couldn't put into words. But she was determined to do right by herself, and by her mother. The monster that had seduced Leanna when she was at her lowest was never worthy of her love.

The days became brisk and the evenings came on sooner. Grace hid her maps and her pennies under a loose floorboard in her room. She kept quiet and didn't go looking for Jimmy, or anyone else, for that matter. Let Teddy think he had broken her. Let him believe he had won. That was the plan, and it seemed to be working.

Grace meekly went about her chores and performed as well as she ever had, smiling, winking, throwing a bit of hip into her swagger across the stage. She worked the audience just like she worked Teddy, becoming everything he wanted her to be, and giving him no reason to complain. His shirts were always clean and neatly folded, his swords were always sharp and shiny. The audience was always charmed. Grace became a model slave.

Teddy had gone from following her daily to once a week, and then less. Grace stayed aware of him and made sure not to pull out her maps on those days. Once he was convinced that her walks were harmless excursions, he left her to get on with them in peace. Grace was careful and thorough. She would not get caught slacking again.

It was six weeks after Teddy had raped her last that she knew she was in even deeper trouble. Her

onthly blood had never come. She wasn't even sure
w she'd managed to keep a pregnancy *this* far, what
th being cut in half at least 3 times since Teddy, well,
ce he'd done that to her. She had no idea if her baby
uld inherit her powers, but she could not chance
other one of Teddy's beatings. She wouldn't allow
yone else to suffer at his monstrous hands, least of all
innocent, unborn child. Grace knew she couldn't let
ddy saw her in half again, or stick those stupid swords
ough her. One wrong move and that unborn baby
uld be in a whole heap of trouble.

She dropped hints and steered him towards
other dismemberment and firewalk show. She'd been
quiet and unassuming recently, that Teddy felt it
ly fair to give in to her obvious desire for what he
sidered an "easy night".

"We'll just do your arms tonight, and a nice
ple firewalk. Later in the week we can build up to
f sawing, the basket trick, *and* a firewalk finale, so this
vn will never forget us."

"They'll never forget us, Teddy, " Grace agreed. It
s obvious to her that tonight would be the night she'd
n waiting for. She'd give them all a show for the ages.

Grace snuck her money and maps down to the
kstage area and hid them in the basket lid that they
uldn't be using tonight. Then she hid a sword in
props, just in case she couldn't get her hand on the
ksaw. She paced around backstage, memorizing her
ape route. There would be no room for mistakes,
en she made her play, it would have to be quick and
rough. Grace rummaged around backstage and found
at and trench coat. She threw these in the corner by the
kstage exit. With any luck she could throw them on
make her escape into the night before anyone really
w what had happened.

Once everything was ready, Grace began setting
for the firewalk that would never happen. She
ributed the sand neatly, and spread out the thin layer
oal. When everything was ready, a strange sense of
n settled over her. Tonight would be the start of the
of her life, one way or the other.

The Mysterious Massimo took the stage to a
sing round of applause. He stood and enjoyed it
just a few seconds, staring out over his adoring
ience with a sense of pride at all that he'd managed
ccomplish. The theater was packed, and they were
hungry for what he was serving them. Mystery, and a
of sadistic pleasure. The Mysterious Massimo bowed
ply and paused, waiting for the clamor to die down.

"I am the Mysterious Massimo, and tonight you
will witness feats beyond your imagination. You will be
amazed and astounded. Yes, tonight, your understanding
of the basic laws of the natural world will be destroyed
and built anew!" He raised his arms as the audience went
wild.

"Witness this, the beautiful, the elegant, the
Lovely Galinda take the stage." At this, Grace walked
onto the stage, waving and smiling at the crowd. The
whoops and cheers rang out. "Watch now, as she puts her
arms into these boxes." He opened a box and showed it
to the crowd from all different angles, ensuring them that
there was no trick to be seen. Grace put her arms inside,
and Massimo closed the lids.

"Watch closely, as I sever these lithe appendages
from their loveliest of hosts!" Massimo pulled out a
hacksaw, and the audience gasped. He sawed the arms
off with a few back and forth motions, all the while
Grace smiled and winked at the audience. Massimo slid
the boxes away from Grace. The audience went utterly
silent. He left the boxes where they were and walked over
towards the coals.

Grace's hands opened their own boxes while
Massimo distracted the audience with his jabber about
her delicate feet and their amazing ability to withstand
the heat. Just as he bent over to light the coals, a single,
dismembered arm hurtled towards him, spurting blood
across the stage while pushing his unbalanced frame
over into the freshly lit coals. He issued forth a surprised
scream and turned to see Grace running towards him, one
arm attached again already and holding a sword. His eyes
went wide as saucers as she slid the sword neatly into his
throat and out the other side. He stood as if to fight back,
and as she pulled the sword back out in a gush of blood,
he looked up in time to see the sword swing at him in a
wide arc. Teddy's smoldering head landed in the lap of a
man in the second row, who tossed it away wildly, then
promptly fainted. Teddy's body crumpled back down to
the coals with a hiss, his clothes now alight.

Grace grabbed her other arm and rushed
backstage, took the bag with her money and map, and
threw on the trench coat and hat. She ran out into the
night, the backdoor slamming shut behind her.

Within the theater, people were screaming and
rushing for the exits. A few men tried to climb the stage
to chase down Grace, but they were hopelessly slow
getting anywhere. One woman stood and retched up her
dinner, while her husband tried desperately to pull her
from their seats. All the while Teddy's body sat upon the
coals, smelling like barbeque.

Grace ran and ran. She could hear the shouting and crying getting quieter as she got further from the theater. Blending into the crowd in her makeshift disguise, if anyone had followed, they didn't know which way she went. She made it to the bus station and got the first bus out of town. Grace sat alone, all the way at the back of the bus. She took a pair of scissors out of her bag and chopped her long waves into a short bob. When the bus stopped in Toledo, Grace went to the first salon she found and asked them to dye her hair black. She bought herself a day dress, then got on the next bus out of town. It took her three more buses to get to New York City.

Once in New York, Grace got herself a room at a youth hostel and got a job in a factory manufacturing garments. It was hard work, but it was honest and Grace chose it herself. It kept her days full, but in the evenings she still kept an eye on the theaters, watching and waiting for the day the Vance juggling troupe would come to town. She wasn't sure what would happen when she found Jimmy again, she just knew that she missed her friend, and he deserved an explanation.

Jimmy stared, shocked, when he saw her. Her short black bob made her look like a completely different person. She wore a champagne colored shift dress with beading around the hips and stockings rolled down just below the hem. Her cloche hat was champagne colored as well, with a black bow. But most disconcerting of all, was her giant baby bump.

"Jimmy!" she cried, and threw her arms around him. "It's so good to see you."

Jimmy searched her face full of smoky kohl and rouge, looking for the girl he knew. "Gracie? Is that really you? When I heard what happened to Teddy, I…"

"Aw, Jimmy, please don't say that name. Don't ever mention him again. He's gone. It's really me. I'm free. No one can hurt me like that now."

"What are you doing in New York, Gracie?"

"Just working in a factory and staying in a hostel until I decide what to do next. I can't work the shows, somebody might recognise me and no one wants to see a pregnant girl perform. Plus, I'm gonna have this baby. I'll put it up for adoption as soon as it's born, but until then, I can't really make a new start."

Jimmy looked at her with his big, sad puppy dog eyes. "Is it… is it *his?*"

Grace looked at Jimmy as if he was mad, "Of course it is, Jimmy. I'd never have. You know, how he was. Had to control me. Had to control everything. Even now, he's in the driver's seat. I coulda let him stab me. He woulda ended it all himself without ever knowing. But I can't hold this baby responsible. I'm gonna sell it to some rich family. It'll have a good life, and then I'll be free."

Jimmy held her close and rubbed her shoulder. "I'm so sorry, Gracie. I'm sorry I wasn't fast enough, or strong enough to save you in time."

"It's okay, Jimmy. I saved myself."

"So what's next, Gracie? Where do you go once you've sold your baby?" Jimmy looked at Grace with a sudden harshness in his eyes.

"Wherever I want, Jimmy. Wherever I damn well please." Grace held his gaze until he dropped it. "I'm not going to apologize. I did what I had to do."

Jimmy nodded. "I know, I know. I just wish things had been different."

"Things are what they are, Jimmy." Grace looked away, she wanted things to be different too. She wanted Jimmy to look at her the way he had before. "You'd better get back to your family, Jimmy. They're waiting for you."

Jimmy flinched as if stung by Grace's dismissal. "See ya round, Gracie," he said, and walked away, leaving her alone.

Gracie decided to keep her baby. She suspected he must be like her to have survived in the first place, and she wouldn't risk him being raised by someone else. Someone who might take advantage of him. Grace named him Joey. Little Joey had Leanna's auburn hair and Teddy's bright blue eyes. Joey rarely cried, even when Gracie wore him swaddled on her back while she worked at the factory for hours on end. He just nuzzled against her napping while she cut fabric and sewed seams.

At home, Grace rocked him and sang, "Hush little Joey, don't you cry." as a little joke. Joey smiled and cooed as Gracie sang her heart out, dancing around the room with him. When September rolled around, Grace counted up her savings and decided it was enough. She didn't want to spend another winter in the cold, working at the factory.

Grace packed up all their important belongings into two small suitcases, swaddled Joey in a blanket and popped him in his pram. They walked down to the train station, and Grace bought a sleeper ticket for California. They boarded the dusty green passenger train, and Grace held Joey on her lap, humming him a little tune. Joey gurgled quietly and snuggled into her arms for a nap.

Grace was unsure what the future held for her and little Joey, but she was eager to find out. Mother and son would take on the world, if they had to. But all she really hoped for was a quiet, happy life, somewhere in the sun.

sleep.

Madi Quinn

She hated them, you know. She looked down on their sleeping forms, as they lay there, unconscious, unknowing, unaware. Contempt for them flared up in her gut like bile, tasting bitter in her mouth and making her even more disgusted. These two, these horrible two, were the most vile, contemptible creatures to tread the earth, and right now, she held a straight razor to the throat of one of them as he slept. His snores echoed off the walls as he remained blissfully unaware of his impending death.

It hadn't always been that way. In truth, she'd once been a well-behaved child; in fact, many had said she was an ideal child, adorable and happy. She'd been born into less than ideal circumstances, to a very young, single mother who'd been suckered in by a manipulative man. The mother's family had rallied around them, helping out where they could assist in raising the child.

However, as time went on, the mother changed, and it wasn't for the better. Most mature as time goes on, but this one didn't seem to do so; quite the opposite, she became more of a child as time passed. When things didn't go her way, she tended to take things out on the child, not in fits of rage, but in ice-cold insults. She would tell the child that the boys would like her much better if she was just a little less heavy, or a little less unattractive. This would be repeated dozens of times a week, until the child began to believe it.

The mother married several times as the years went on, always spur-of-the-moment affairs, with men that were ambiguous about their feelings at best, and usually negligent to hostile towards the child. Then, along came the last one, the final stepfather, the last candidate for co-dependency. To say he was unintelligent was an understatement; he was a complete idiot, but he was a malignant idiot, a man too stupid to realize how stupid he actually was. He also had a nasty habit of thinking himself a clever con man, frequently trying to skim off his employers, and always getting caught. He'd been blacklisted from almost every employer he was qualified to work for as a thief and cheat, and then had the nerve to blame everyone but himself. Unfortunately, this also contributed to him having a massive ego and a hair-trigger temper, both of which were constantly tested by the child.

The mother had met him while she had been working for a prison outreach program, and he had been an inmate. He never specified what he had been incarcerated for, and she never really wanted to know. They became friends, bonding over a mutual love of Christ, chocolate, and not having their children around. Of course, eventually he was released, and they had to return to their normal lives. They then had to inform their families of each other's existence. It was, of course, a bit of a shock to his wife and children, but her child, the child of which we've been speaking, wasn't told until he showed up on their doorstep, backpack stuffed with clothes and a smile on his face.

She wasn't pleased, but she could do nothing. She was shouted down and sent to her room. Thus began a campaign of marginalization and degradation that would go on for many years, leading into her teens. She would spend time in her room, leave to go to school or to her friends' houses, and stay away from the house for almost the entire weekend with her boyfriend (or occasionally, her girlfriend; she wasn't particular). Whenever she was anywhere near her parents (which she had no choice to call them, as he demanded to be called her father, and her actual father was long gone), war would break out, and the shouting could be heard by neighbors who would sometimes feel compelled to call the police.

The child was well-known by juvenile officers, unfortunately; she had been picked up for shoplifting more than once. It wasn't because she just felt like it, but because she felt she couldn't get clothes any other way. Getting her parents to spend any money on her was like pulling teeth with telekinesis. It simply wasn't going to happen, so the girl had little choice but to steal what she needed. It was still a crime, a crime she was guilty of more than once, but one she'd gotten terrifyingly good at, learning quickly how to look however she wanted without actually being noticed. She wasn't slender by any measure, but still managed to be able to sneak up on just about anyone. She was managing to hold down a job working at a local grocery store and would often be able to sneak up behind her co-workers and surprise them, even when they knew she was around. It was a useful skill, to be a bigger girl with brightly colored hair and ripped jeans, and still be able to move without drawing people's attention. It was at this point she started to formulate the idea that would bring her to this point, where we met her.

She hated them, you see. They traumatized her, they brutalized her into submission, but they could never break her will. They only fed the fire of hatred and vengeance and honed the razor's edge. Though it was pitch black, she'd waited in the darkness of her tomb-like bedroom in the basement. She liked the crypt atmosphere there; Death was a comrade to her, not something to be feared. Tonight, she would give Death a gift that she'd longed to give him for years; these snoring bastards would finally bleed and die at her command. Her only regret was that she would not see the life fade from their eyes as they perished; for the sake of her final liberation, it needed to remain dark.

She stood over him, waiting, holding the straight razor, and wanting to pull the razor across his thickl[y] bearded throat. She paused, her hand not wanting t[o] move. Though he looked like little more than a savag[e], a Neanderthal to her, she almost pitied him. He wa[s] a prideful, cretinous beast, but he was also hapless. H[e] could never be more than he was, and he was about to b[e] robbed of any chance of redemption. Suddenly she wa[s] keenly aware of what sort of power she now possesse[d] she alone, in this moment, held complete dominion ov[er] this worm's life. She alone had utter control over wheth[er] he even had a future or not. She, and by extension h[er] razor, were God Almighty as far as that pile of steamin[g] shit was concerned, and only she could decide if he live[d] or died. Not some bearded, old voyeur in the clouds, n[ot] some vague, nameless concept of deity, not some middl[e] age Jewish carpenter. It was *her* and only her.

And she chose. Her hand glided with minimal effo[rt] back towards her body with a sickening slicing sound, an[d] the snore turned into a series of wet gurgles, and then f[ell] silent forever.

She remained silent and still for just a mome[nt] waiting to see if the mother was going to wake, expecti[ng] a fight, but astoundingly enough, the mother remain[ed] asleep. Prince Valium continuing to faithfully hold vig[il] She walked slowly around the bed, now starting to becom[e] slick with the blood of the future maggot colony laying [on] the side nearest the bathroom, trying hard not to step in t[he] substance she was sure would give her hepatitis. She cre[pt] around to the opposite side of the bed and looked down [at] the mother, feeling thirteen years of emotion well up insi[de] her stomach like a bad sandwich. She'd always heard th[at] once you'd done your first, it got easier, but like with se[x] it was all bullshit. Sex still hurt after the first time a[nd] killing was still hard to do after the first one, even if th[ey] deserved it.

She took the razor and held it inches above t[he] mother's throat, trying not to think of the woman [as] *her* mother. No, she'd relinquished *that* distinction t[he] moment she'd decided to forsake her child's well-being [in]

e sake of her own amusement. She'd earned this when
e'd taken a monster on as an attack dog against her own
ild. This *had* to happen. She deserved it.

So why was it so hard to to do? She wrestled with
e choice in her mind far more than she had with the
eat sack that lay bleeding and defecating next to them.
oughts ran through her mind without her consent,
oughts of happy times in her early childhood, running
d playing, laughing, and dancing, leaping into piles of
ow or leaves, and through it all she was happy. Concerts
th her band, or her choir, or performances of the school
y that she was intensely proud of, where the crowds
dly applauded.

But the mother was not involved in any of them.
e was never involved; she never cared to be involved.
e child's grandmother and aunts would show up and hug
, or bundle her up for winter playtime, but the mother
s never there. In fact, the mother never seemed to do
ything except berate her, and inform her of where she
s wrong, or even worse, pray for her soul, as she'd
len so far from the glory of…

No. No more.

Rage filled her soul, welling up from the pit of her
mach like burning bile, and she leapt atop the mother,
ddling her, and pinning her shoulders to the bed with
knees. The mother stirred from her sleep, her eyes
pping wide open once she realized what was going on.
e child clapped her hand tightly over the mother's nose
mouth before she could scream, a sadistic grin on her
e as the mother tried to struggle uselessly to get away.

The child looked into the mother's eyes, their
cold blue seeming far colder than usual, an almost
psychopathic lack of pathos reflecting back a lifetime
of neglect. "No, no, no, we can't have you screaming,
MOM," the child hissed, barely above a whisper. She
drove one of the corner points of the straight razor into
the mother's throat, causing the mother to whimper, but
making her stop moving immediately.

"Now. You might feel a bit of wetness. I can
assure you that's not Daddy pissing the bed again, if you
get my meaning. You are going to join him, but only when
I say. You have no power. Not anymore. It's not about
you anymore. *Your* story is done. I wanted you to know
that *I* beat you. I wanted you to know that *I* won. He was
worthless, useless, just a pile of shit, just like every other
pile of shit you hooked up with, but you…"

The child lifted the blade of the razor, running it
down the side of the mother's face slowly, as she bent
down to whisper quietly in the mother's ear. "…the boys
would like you so much better if you were dead." The
child pulled the blade quickly and quietly across her
mother's throat, from carotid to carotid, savoring the sound
of parting flesh and gushing blood, reveling in the choking
and gurgling as the little bit of light in her mother's eyes
faded into nothing.

The house burned to the ground that night, leaving
little behind in the way of evidence beyond two charred
corpses, burnt so badly that the fire was declared the cause
of death. In town, most (including the police) believed
that the man had a shady deal go wrong, and it had led to
their death and the kidnapping of the child. There could
have been no other possibility that made any sense. Surely
the child wouldn't have been capable of anything like that,
after all.

Would she?

THE GIRL WHO DREAMED TOO LOUD
BY SN HUMPHREYS

Grace ran full pelt down the stairs, skipping steps, eyes wide and breath ragged. It had felt like this countless times before and surely would again forever and ever and ever. Fear gripped her chest, squeezing the air from her lungs, as she realized the steps just kept going and she wasn't getting any closer to the bottom. Behind her she could feel the weight of the witch's stare, boring holes into her back, willing her to trip and fall. She couldn't go on like this. Suddenly she *did* trip, and then she was falling into the endless inky black, and the witch was all around her laughing and tearing at her hair and skin with invisible claws.

Grace sat up in bed shaking and quietly sobbing. Even in sleep she couldn't escape.

Grace was 8 years old and couldn't wait to be 18. *Everything's better when you're grown up*, she thought, sitting in her room, admiring her sticker album. *Grown ups are never afraid.* Not of the kinds of things Grace feared, anyway.

Grace had lots of sticker albums, some were full of foil stickers, some fuzzy stickers. This one was her scratch and sniff stickers. The last three pages, the ones she was studying lovingly, were full of her two favorite scents, root beer and popcorn. The scents mingled together and instantly transported her to the movie theater. The big, scratchy chairs, the cold whirr of the air conditioning, the sticky floors and the way she could hear the soles of her shoes peeling off the with each step. Grace loved the theater, and she loved movies. Her favorite was Tron, but she also liked animated movies, action movies, and comedies. She liked films where the good guys came out on top, and everything had a happy ending. Anything but scary movies. There was enough fear in Grace's life. She took one last sniff of the shiny, well-loved book then closed up and placed it on top of her dresser.

Grace was an only child, and as such everything was just as she liked it. Dinner was always something Grace wanted to eat. She picked all the shows she watched. Her toys wer exactly where she left them and never got lost o misplaced or broken. Grace liked her quiet and couldn't really imagine having to share her spa or time with someone else's needs or desires. S wasn't particularly good at sharing, because sh never really had to.

Grace looked around at the bubblegum pink walls of her room. It was a bit of a mess, usual. Her room reflected the inner landscape her mind quite accurately, in that way. Toys an coloring books strewn around the room, clothe tossed on the floor carelessly. Grace picked them up and stuffed them into her white wicke hamper as a token gesture towards some sort of order. She yawned and stretched and headed downstairs.

The staircase made her nervous. Her mother blamed this reluctance on a fall she'd taken a few years back, while running up the

airs. Her feet flew out from under her and
er chin hit each step on the way down. There
as a scar on the bottom of her chin from that
ay, a lumpy line that she rubbed when she was
inking very hard.

The truth was Grace always felt watched
n those stairs. She was sure that some horrid,
rinkled old crone appeared behind her every
me she walked down them. And when she
alked up them, it was crouching just out of
iew, waiting to jump out and grab her at the top.
he invisible observer placed herself in Grace's
ind's eye, watching with intention, sending
ivers of fear down her spine.

It was Saturday morning, so she got
erself a bowl of cereal and sat down in front
the television, ready for some cartoons. She
runched her toes into the shaggy brown carpet,
tting in front of the flickering screen, munching
way on her Fruity Pebbles, thinking about
thing but exactly what problem the lions would
ce on this episode of Voltron. Grace's mother
as in the kitchen, washing dishes and humming.

"Don't forget to put your bowl in the sink
hen you're done," her mom said, "I'm going
stairs to shower."

Grace was putting her bowl away when
l the hairs on her body pricked up at attention.
oldness washed over her. She felt eyes–hungry,
human eyes–boring holes in her back. She
rned towards the slatted doors that housed
e water heater, staring at where she was sure
mething lurked. The boiler hissed and rattled
d banged, and Grace ran into the living room
aking.

Grace rode her bike to the little park a few
ocks down from her house. She'd brought a
ce box and a book, but for once, she didn't
el like reading. The sun was shining and the
ayground was empty, except for a little league
am practicing on the baseball diamond at the
end. Grace ran over to the swingset and threw

herself into the task of pumping her legs to see
how high she could get before the turning in her
stomach transformed itself from elation into fear.
She didn't know what it was that drove her to go
too high. Pushing through the feelings of joy and
freedom until it all became too much, too high,
and the cold fear set in. Then she would stop
kicking, and let her feet drag in the dirt below,
slowing the swing to a standstill. She always ran
to the swings, and went through the exact same
motions, pushing herself past her limit every
time.

The bathroom left Grace feeling alone and
vulnerable. She'd heard stories of Bloody Mary,
who would appear in the mirror and grab your
soul or scratch your eyes out. In the stories you
had to chant her name, but Grace felt sure that if
she just thought it hard enough, the spirit would
hear her anyway, and heed her call. Whenever
she looked in the mirror, instead of seeing her
own reflection, it felt more like something was
looking back. It sent a prickly sensation down her
spine. Grace washed her hands quickly and went
back downstairs, a bit shaky, her stomach in a
tight knot.

The dark, empty bathrooms, mirrors
standing like portals, and dancing spirits and
ghosts haunted Grace at every waking moment.
The void of the unknown darkened her every
step. Sleep provided no relief for all of the
nightmares that swallowed her, and sleepless
nights wondering what lurked under her bed or
just outside the door gave no respite. Dark murky
depths of water, heights, and danger lurked just
behind her, ready to consume her. Yet, more than
that, the distrust and fear of her own mind and
an inability to separate the curtain between what
was real and what was imaginary enveloped her
to the point of no escape. No safety.

Dinner was tuna casserole, one of her
favorites. Grace dug in, avoiding all the bits of

mushroom with practiced ease and slurping up the creamy sauce with a sense of joy. Her mother was there, and with the TV blaring away in the other room as they ate, not to mention a blessedly silent water heater, a sense of calm–a sliver of respite–came to her. Grace finished her dish and put her bowl in the sink.

"Go upstairs and get ready for your bath", her mom said, "I'll run the water."

Grace lingered at the foot of the stairs. The hallway leading off towards the front door extended beyond it, ending in a dark corner that housed the cat's litter box. She stared off into the blackness, hoping not to see anything untoward in the shadows. She turned and took to the stairs, repeating that nothing was there over and over in her head as the sickening ball of lead formed in her belly once again. At the top of the staircase she flicked on the hall light, eyes darting in every direction. Her rising panic began to ease as she stepped into her room.

Grace went to her dresser and dug around until she found her Super Girl nightgown, which she laid out on her bed. She heard her mother running the bath, and began to strip off her clothes, tossing them in her hamper.

"Bubbles, please!" she called out. Baths were the only time she enjoyed being in the bathroom.

"Okay, okay." her mother answered with a laugh.

Grace put on her green robe and walked down the hallway towards the bathroom. She dropped her robe at the door and climbed into the relaxing bubble bath. She dunked her hair under the water, immersed herself, then raided the bath caddy for toys to play with. She grabbed a pink haired Jem doll and dunked her under the soapy water.

"Truly outrageous." she giggled.

Grace played with her toys and made bubble beards until her mother called up the stairs and told her it was time to get out. She dried off, put on her robe and brushed her teeth. She stared at the patterns in the bathroom tiles, searching for forms like people liked to do with clouds. She found a beautiful ballerina, doing a pirouette. Grace smiled and spat a mouthful of foam into the sink. She wiped off her face and headed back to her bedroom to read.

Grace lost time, completely transported into the world of her book, <u>The Witch Of Blackbird Pond</u>, oblivious to everything going o around her. Before she knew it, her mother was there, telling her good night.

"Can I have my TV on for a bit?" Grace asked hopefully.

"Sure, honey." Her mother switched the small black and white television on her dresser on. "Don't stay up too late. We're going to Nanny's tomorrow."

"Good night, mom. Love you."

"Love you too, Gracie. Sleep tight."

Grace's mother switched off the light and left the room. Grace listened to her footfalls on the stairs and looked around her room. Everything took on a sinister cast that she didn' trust in the dark. She pulled the blanket up to her chin and tried to pay attention to the TV, ignoring the chill climbing her spine. Every cree of the old house set her teeth on edge. *What doe 'sleep tight' even mean, anyway?* Grace willed herself to be sleepy. She stared at the bedroom door, waiting for it to creek open. She was sure it wouldn't if she was looking at it, so she kept staring. Eventually her eyes fluttered closed.

That night Grace dreamed the witch was after her. She never saw her face, but she somehow knew it was ancient and wrinkled up like a paper ball. That feeling of something watching washed over her dream self like a col veil, and she ran out of the house, and into her mother's old brown car. She willed herself sma so small that the witch couldn't see her, and because it was a dream, it worked. She shrunk down until the dust in the air looked like beach

lls floating around her. The witch was close,
t even her magic was not enough to find Grace,
o hid herself under a magazine on the back
at. The witch receded, but Grace could feel that
e would wait forever if she had to. The witch
d nothing if not time.

Grace awoke, groggy. She got dressed,
en went to the bathroom and brushed her teeth,
 tired to fret about the mirror and what might
 lurking in it. She remembered every bit of
r dream. She searched for the ballerina in the
es but couldn't remember exactly which whirl
color she'd found her in. Grace gave up, and
aded downstairs, stiff with the expectation of
ing watched, but the feeling didn't come. She
rried down anyway.

"Grace, how would you like some donuts
 breakfast?" her mother called from the
chen.

"Ooh, yes please!" Grace chirped, perking
ht up at the idea.

Grace's mother brushed her waist length
k hair and swept it up into pigtails. Then
ace put on her shoes and they bundled out the
or and into the car. Grace eyed the backseat
membering her dream.

"So, how did you sleep last night? You left
 TV on all night again." her mother asked.

"I slept okay." Grace lied. She rarely
red her nightmares with her mother, or anyone
e. Grace felt like talking about the things she
agined made them more real, and they were
eady real enough. "Can I get a French cruller
d a hot chocolate?"

"Sure sweetie, of course you can."

The donut shop had slightly dirty floor
eiling windows all the way around. It was
t on the highway, in the middle of a dull gray
king lot. They sat at a small table and Grace
ing her legs back and forth as she ate her
ut. She adored French crullers. The sticky
et sugar coating clung to her finger tips. She
licked her fingers clean as she watched the cars
pass by.

Grace's grandparents were only past the
park with the duck pond Poppy liked to take her
to. When they passed it, Grace knew they were
almost there. Her grandparents had recently
become very religious. Grace didn't understand
why they had to change religions, or what was so
bad about their old one. Now there were always
bibles strewn about the house (they had *lots* of
bibles) and tapes of sermons blaring from their
stereo whenever Grace came round to see them.
They were always telling Grace's mother that if
she didn't convert, she'd wind up in hell.

One winter morning, Nan's car wouldn't
start. Everyone was outside, scraping their
windshields free of the frost, getting ready to
leave for school and work. Grace's nan lifted the
hood of the car, and began to shout. "Get thee
out of my engine Satan, in Jesus's name, I rebuke
thee!" The neighbors put their heads down and
ignored the old woman's shouting. Grace sank
lower in the passenger seat and tried to hide
her face. Nan went on shouting and banging on
the hood for a solid five minutes before the car
finally started and they drove off.

Every time they visited, Nan would make
tea and coffee, then suggest a church visit for
Grace's mom while sliding her coffee in front of
her. The pitch was always the same. "Grace is
already saved. I've prayed and prayed to Jesus,
and she *will* be born again. If you don't start
coming to our church, and accept the lord as your
savior, you will not be in heaven with her when
she dies." All of this with Grace sitting at the
table, stuffing her face with whatever tasty dish
her nan had prepared for her.

"I like my church." was all Mom would
say, and not long after she would start making
excuses– we have homework to do, or Grace has
music lessons– and they would get up and leave
for home.

Grace loved her grandparents very much,

and was happy to go visit them, even though things had become weird. Nan always made her something nice to eat, baked ziti or chicken parmesan were staples. They had cable TV because that's where the religious stations were, so Grace could go in the other room and watch the cartoon channels or even the music one if she kept the volume reasonably low. They used to live in a big house in a nice neighborhood, with a large backyard where Grace had an above ground swimming pool, and her own room. But then their clothing shop went out of business. Now they lived in a little house just next to a big storage business which they managed right on the highway. It was small and loud, and everything outside was dirty and gray, but none of it really mattered to Grace. What she really hoped for was for her grandparents to be happy. Their arguments were frequent, and violent. Once Grace came in from playing outside to witness a glass ashtray fly past the door and strike the wall. She backed slowly out and closed the door on their shouts and sat outside nursing a sudden onset migraine, feeling like someone had just stepped over her grave. Grace had to admit there was less of that sort of thing since they'd changed religions. Now all their anger was channeled into casting out demons and judging the not-yet-saved.

Grace's nan gave her a hug in the doorway as their miniature apricot poodle jumped around their feet. Blossom had been with them a year now. She gave her poppy a kiss on the cheek, then sat on the floor in the living room petting the dog. The grown ups sat in the kitchen drinking coffee and talking. Grace only half listened to their conversation. Grown up conversations were boring anyway. Blossom rolled over onto her back and Grace dutifully rubbed her belly.

Time passed slowly, the air filled with the droning sounds of conversation from the next room. Grace climbed up on the green velvet plastic covered couch and stared at the walls of her grandparents' living room. There were crosses, and family photos, and a large, hard wood cabinet filled with porcelain statues and crystal tchotchkes. Blossom laid curled up by her feet as Grace drifted off to sleep. She dreamed she was in a green field, with daisies and dandelions dotted all around her. She knelt in the grass, picking flowers in the warm sun. A gray cloud passed over and there was a sudden chill in the air, a violin played a haunting, squeaky tune. Train tracks, old rickety ones came up through the soil, under Grace's knees. She tried to move, but couldn't. She pulled at her legs with her hands, desperate with fear, but they wouldn't budge. Grace looked up to see a big black steam engine bearing down on her at full speed.

Nanny shook her shoulder. "Do you want some tea, Grace? It's almost time to go and we've barely seen you."

On the car ride home Grace got to choose the radio station. Eighties new wave blared from the speakers, and Grace and her mom sang along.

"Tainted love, woah oh, tainted love." Grace loved these moments, singing happily while watching the world pass by out the passenger side window, her hair blowing around her face.

Back at the house Grace ran up to her room, eager to return to her book. She was a fast reader, and was already almost half way through The Witch of Blackbird Pond. Grace identified with Kit, the main character and was curious about all the politics of Puritan New England. It all seemed so rigid and backwards, but very like something her Nan would have approved of. Grace continued reading while she ate her dinner. By bedtime she'd devoured the book.

Once again, Grace lay in the dark with her little black and white TV casting the only light in the room. Some late night talk show was on, but Grace was distracted by the shadows. Everything seemed to vibrate in the dark, like it was charged ith electricity. Grace stared off towards the doorway, expecting something to appear, but nothing did. Eventually sleep overtook her.

This time she was on a stage. The lights were hot and bright. She couldn't see the audience, but she could feel their hungry gaze, waiting for something to happen. Grace tried to stand, then realized she was in a box, with just her head, arms and feet sticking out. There was horrible, out of tune organ music playing. Her insides squirmed. Then a man in a singed magician's outfit appeared next to her. He had piercing blue eyes but all his hair was burnt away. When he smiled, his teeth looked like knife points. His skin looked like candle wax about to melt. He held a great long hacksaw. He bowed to the unseen audience, and then sawed the box.

Wood shavings flew everywhere. *That's not how this trick works!* Thought Grace, but he kept sawing right through the box, and then through Grace's middle. She waited for the pain, but it was a ghost. She could feel the presence of the saw, parting her insides, she could feel them spilling out, but only in a numb sort of way. Somehow, this horrified her more than the possible pain. The melting man looked at her, directly in her eyes. Recognition shot through her like an electric impulse, waking her up.

Time to get ready for school. Grace got dressed, all bleary eyed and took herself downstairs for her morning cereal. Her mother was in the kitchen, putting together Grace's lunch in a rush. She started work at nine, and left before Grace caught the bus to school.

"Good morning, Grace" her mother was always perky in the morning. "Lunch is on the counter. Don't forget your key and have a great day!"

"Morning." Grace grunted.

"I've got to go, traffic is going to be bad this morning. Love you!" Grace's mother rushed out the door.

"Bye, mom." Grace dug into her cereal while her brain struggled to get the hang of being awake. Mornings were always hard for her, everything seemed so bright and loud. She put her bowl in the sink then trudged back up the stairs to brush her teeth.

Halfway up the stairs, the telltale coldness washed over her. Grogginess replaced with terror and wakefulness, she froze. Six more steps, she thought to herself. Grace would not look behind her, sure that she would see something terrible if she did.

Grace's eyes never left the mirror while she brushed her teeth. She thought about opening the medicine cabinet so she wouldn't have to look at it, but then she was sure something would appear behind her when she closed it, so she skipped that plan entirely. Sometimes Grace wondered if it was normal to be this afraid all the time. Other kids never talked about it, and they all seemed fine in situations where Grace was practically frozen with fear.

There was no escaping it, Grace was going to have to walk back down those stairs, and shut off the hall light before she did it. Grace steeled herself, then flipped the switch. Her nerves were already toast, so she took the stairs two at a time, hand gliding along the bannister. Adrenaline rushed through her as she ran into the living room and collected her bag and key. She'd have to walk past them again to get out of the house. She wasn't looking forward to that, but it was almost time to go.

Her tabby cat, Rascal, laid on the couch staring at her, the racket from Grace running down the stairs having disturbed him. Grace walked over and scratched him behind the ear. She still felt she was being watched. That rarely happened in the living room, and now she was afraid to turn around. Her arms were covered in goosebumps.

Grace walked into the kitchen to grab her lunch, then to the front door, furtively glancing up the stairs as she passed. She opened the door, suddenly hit with the surety that the witch would appear behind it as soon as she did. She rushed outside and slammed the door behind her, locking it with a sigh of relief, and ran down to catch the bus.

Grace was first to the bus stop. She waved hello to the crossing guard and leaned up against the chain link fence, waiting for her heartbeat to slow down. Other children soon followed her, and their idle chatter helped her calm down. That sense of being watched never completely left her, though it seemed smaller, quieter.

The morning was long and monotonous. Grace drew pictures in the margins of her notes as her mind wandered. She tried to pay attention, but it rarely worked. Mostly she daydreamed throughout class and hoped the information stuck in her brain somehow. Usually, it did.

She sat at the end of the table at lunchtime. Jamie scanned the table with big round eyes, then finally said, "Did anyone see the fashion show episode of Jem at the weekend?"

"I felt *so bad* for Shana until she got all the credit for everyone's outfits!" Ellen answered. Suddenly the table resembled nothing so much as a coop full of chickens clucking back and forth. Grace picked at her food, too tired to add to the conversation, even though she'd watched the episode as well. When the girls all bundled out the door for recess, she hung back. Grace wasn't in the mood for idle chatter, or tag, or wall ball. She decided to sit under the big oak at the far end of the playground, digging at the dirt with a stick and watching the others at play. Grace's friends chattered on as they walked around the playground, oblivious to her absence.

Grace heard a blood curdling scream.

It was Nathan, a boy in her class. It looked like he'd run directly into the old tree stump about ten yards away from where she sat. His leg was bent at a weird angle, and cut open from his lower thigh in a diagonal slash right across his knee and down his lower leg. The skin hung in wet, thick flaps and the bone was exposed to her view. Nathan's face was twisted in pain, and Grace stared on mute with shock.

"Grace!" Mr. Garret shouted over to her, "Go tell the nurse, quick as you can."

Grace got up and ran to the school. The other children were all wandering slowly toward the boy who'd fallen, asking Grace what she'd seen. She ignored them and ran up the stairs to the building two at a time. She hurried inside, doors banging shut behind her. The nurse's office was at the center of the building, and Grace rushed down the hallway, heart beating in her throat. The image of Nathan's bloody knee cap flashing through her mind.

"Why are you running?" The nurse stood up from her desk.

"The big tree stump." Grace huffed out the words in a breathless jumble, " Nathan fell. There's lots of blood. I think I saw his bone. Mr Garret said…"

The nurse had grabbed a first aid kit and was bundling out of the room before Grace finished. She was at the far end of the hallway by the time Grace had collected herself to follow. Grace watched her stride hurriedly along and finally unclenched. The nurse turned and looked at her.

"Go to the office and ask them to call 911. Tell them what you saw." She turned on her heel and headed back towards the playground.

Grace ran down the hall in the other direction until she got to the front office to tell the receptionist. The bell rang.

"Get back to class, Grace, I'll take it from here."

By the time she had reached her desk, Grace could hear the sirens. They sounded like they were a million miles away. The journey to

r classroom was like walking through soup,
r limbs thick and heavy and hard to move. The
 seemed tense as Mr. Garret told them to open
eir science books to page 130 and read the
apter. His face was as white as the page, Grace
ought, and was somehow glad she was not
ne in feeling terrified by what she'd seen. For
ce. She tried to push the gory scene out of her
ind and read.

On the bus ride home, everyone was
king about Nathan. Kids in other classes
essed people for info, their eyes shining with
nger for details. Grace sat at the front of the
s and averted her gaze from everyone. She
n't want to talk about it, she was still trying to
 the picture out of her head. Her own demons
re far from her thoughts for a change.

Grace got off the bus and walked home.
e sat down on the steps and sobbed. She cried
 Nathan and his horrible bloody leg, yes, but
 also cried for herself. For her fear and her
pelessness that things would ever change.
me kids she knew walked past, and before they
ld see her crying, she pulled herself together
 went inside.

It was more than an hour before her mother
uld get home. Grace fixed herself a snack and
 down at the kitchen table to get started on
 homework. Every once in a while the water
ter would make a noise and her eyes would
 over to the closet, but the feeling didn't
ne. She plugged away at her math problems
il she heard a key in the door.

Grace ran out into the living room to
lcome her mother home. She looked tired,
eated even.

"Hi, Grace," her mother tried to muster up
ne brightness to her voice, but Grace could tell
'd had a bad day.

"Hi, mom. How was your day?"

Her mother sighed. "It was fine. How was
r day?"

Grace thought about telling her mother
everything that had happened, but looking at her
haggard expression, she just couldn't add to it.

"It was fine, mom. I'm just finishing up my
math homework."

"That's good, honey. I'll start dinner in a
minute."

Grace finished up her math and packed her
books back into her backpack. She left the bag
next to the couch and took herself up to her room
to wait for dinner.

That night, Grace's dreams were full of the
faceless witch. This one picked up where the last
had left off, she was shrunken and hiding in the
backseat of her mother's car. Her mom got in and
started driving silently, without looking back, and
Grace slowly returned to her normal size. The
hag was right behind them. Grace wasn't sure
how she knew, but she did. She tried to tell her
mother to drive faster, but she couldn't open her
mouth. A voice laughed in her head. *What's the
matter, poppet? Can't speak?*

Grace woke in the middle of the night.
Adrenaline coursed through her. She stared off
at the darkened doorway. Her mother hadn't left
the hall light on. Grace reached over and turned
her TV on, leaving the volume off. Somehow
the light from the TV made everything around it
seem darker. She tossed and turned and tried to
get back to sleep.

Morning came, and Grace felt as though
someone had wedged an ice pick into her eye and
through her brain, ready to lobotomise her. Her
mother called up the school.

"Looks like another migraine. Yes, she's
scheduled for an MRI next week. Thank you."
Her mother hung up the phone. "Go back up to
bed, Grace. I'll try to get the day off of work."

Grace's headaches had become so frequent
that her doctor had ordered a bunch of tests.
She'd missed a lot of school, and on the days
when she was there, she was a frequent guest in
the nurse's office. Sometimes her mother couldn't

get off work and Grace would spend the day alone, usually on the couch downstairs with her pillows and blanket. For now she lay in bed with her forehead pressed up against the cool wall and the curtains drawn to keep out as much light as possible.

"I'll be home today, Grace, " her mother said softly from the doorway, "Just call me if you need anything." Grace grunted in response and fell into a dreamless sleep.

Grace woke to the smell of food. She put on her green robe and padded down the stairs, stomach rumbling.

"What time is it?" she asked her mother, rubbing her eyes

"Dinner time. Are you hungry?" Grace's mum set a bowl on the table, filled with the pasta "chili" that she loved. It was just elbow macaroni, with ground beef, corn, and spices, but for Grace it was the ultimate comfort food.

"Yes, please." She mumbled and dug into her dinner. Her headache was dull now, less like the stabbing feeling it had been that morning. Grace's mom set a baby aspirin pill next to her juice glass.

"Take this when you're done eating."

Grace finished her dinner and took the pill. She was not hopeful that it would help, but she took it anyway.

"Are you up for a little TV?" Grace's mother asked, "I'll go get your pillows and you can lay down here on the couch.

"Sure." Grace got out her blanket while her mom ran upstairs for the pillows. Once she'd gotten comfortable, she fell right back to sleep.

This time she dreamed. She was lying on the floor in front of the television. She had her pillows and her green blanket and her mother was on the big couch, on the far side of the room, directly behind her. There was a commercial on. Suddenly the room seemed to grow. The distance between her and her mother was like that of an ocean. A man-shaped shadow fell over her. It was the burnt man again, his clothes still barely alight, his skin now less wax like and more like hot red tissue, the fresh skin burned away. He bent down to whisper in her ear, his fiery breath pricking up the hairs on her arms.

Grace, I'm going to have to take your heart. You aren't using it anyway, are you?

Suddenly he was in front of the television, his tall frame silhouetted by the light. *Maybe I will peel your skin like an onion.* He reached towards her chest with his long, clawed fingers. She felt surprisingly little as his claws pierced her flesh. The smell of barbequed meat filled her nose.

Grace woke up to find the sun shining in through the window. Her mother was asleep on the other couch. It was almost time to get ready for school. Grace went into the kitchen and got herself a glass of orange juice. Her headache was mostly gone and she'd have to go to school today. She finished off her drink and went upstairs to get dressed.

Grace got ready for school, brushing her teeth, changing her clothes and brushing her hair. She put her hair up in a crooked ponytail and headed back downstairs. This time the feeling of being watched washed over her before she took a single step. The hairs on her arms stood up and she shivered. She tried to take the stairs slowly, carefully, but she felt hot breath on the back of her neck and lost her grip entirely. She ran down the stairs and jumped down the last three. Her mother sat up on the couch in alarm.

"Grace?" she called out.

"I'm right here. Sorry for waking you. It time to get up." The alarm clock upstairs started to sound.

"Oh, okay" Grace's mother mumbled. "Guess you're feeling better today."

Grace's dreams were rarely good. There were nightly visits from the hag. Grace hid erself anywhere she could, shrinking down, making herself invisible. Each night the hag crept closer, sometimes Grace felt her breath prick up the little hairs on the back of her neck. The singed man found new tricks to torture and mutilate Grace's body with. He stabbed her, cut off her limbs, and set her on fire, all the while, the invisible audience whooped and cheered. Nathan ran through her dreams, right toward the big tree stump head turned to look at whoever chased him. Grace tried to call out to him, but her voice stuck in her throat. His foot hit a root and he went flying, his face sporting an O of surprise as the jagged stump ripped through the meat of his leg. His eyes met hers, his glance accusing. The only halfway decent dreams she had was when she dreamed she had super strength. She could catch the villain and pummel him with her powerful fists, punching and punching until she knocked him clear out of sight. All this power left her uneasy, burdened with the knowledge that she was completely unworthy of the gift.

Another new nightmare came too. In this one she was sitting on a couch talking to a woman who didn't look like her mother, but was her mother in the dream. She had long, wavy black hair like Grace, and a pale, angular face. The woman stared at her with enormous black eyes, like pools of nothing, deep and foreboding.

You have something on your face, Grace.

The woman's face got closer, her eyes and smile growing wider. Unnaturally wide.

Something that belongs to me…

The woman's hand reached up towards her face, her eyes huge and her smile gaping, full of razor sharp teeth. Too many teeth. Grace awoke.

It was the day of Grace's MRI appointment. Her mother had taken off from work, and they went to the donut shop for breakfast. Grace's stomach rumbled and her hands shook.. She'd never had an MRI before. Her mother told her it was like a giant magnet that she'd be inside, and if she was very, very still, it wouldn't take too long. Grace picked at her french cruller and tried not to worry too much about it.

The MRI machine was big and white and sterile. The whole room like some antiseptic scene from a sci-fi movie. Grace lay on the table and tried to get comfortable as she was warned, once again, to lie perfectly still. Before she knew it the table was retracting inside. Luckily, Grace didn't mind small spaces. She concentrated on laying still as the machine banged and whirred. After a few minutes, she fell asleep.

Soon Grace woke to the machine spitting her out in slow motion.

"Your neurologist should call you to talk about the results in the next week or so," the technician said. Grace wondered what kind of weirdness they would find going on in her brain. Would they be able to see anything that could explain her headaches, her near constant fear, or would it just look like a normal brain, keeping its secrets in its deep folds?

That night Grace dreamed she was in the MRI machine. The knocking and whirring came faster, louder. The machine began to shake. She felt a hand caress her arm, the skin thin and dry as paper tissue. Suddenly it gripped her arm tightly. *Grace,* it nearly shouted in her ear.

Grace sat up, covered in sweat and shaking. She searched the dark for the eyes she felt on her, the phantom hand of the hag, but there was nothing there. Grace sobbed quietly in the dark. She felt those eyes watching her, and they were pleased.

On the weekends, Grace played softball for a local team, Black Cat Propane. They were a decent team, they'd placed 3rd the year before and looked likely to again this year. She had started off as an outfielder, but this season the coach had asked her to start as a catcher. It was a very different position, but Grace gave it her all. She felt like it was a lot of responsibility. She had to keep eyes out for anyone trying to steal bases, anticipate what her pitcher was going to do, and try not to get hit by the bat when the hitter actually connected with the ball. It took a lot more focus than standing around in the outfield waiting for a ball to get hit that far out.

Grace enjoyed playing, but was happiest when there was no one in the stands she knew to watch her. She felt this overwhelming expectation to perform whenever she was watched, and didn't want to disappoint anyone with a bad showing. Grace was constantly worried about how she was perceived by others. She was preoccupied with the idea of being found lacking somehow.

The park they were playing at was Grace's favorite. It was on the far side of town, and the boy that Grace liked lived nearby. He would come and watch whenever they played there. His name was Tony, and he went to a different school, so these games were the only time Grace got to see him. He had dark hair and big blue eyes. Some of the girls on her team went to his school, so they would chat with him, and Grace was glad because it gave him an excuse to stay around. She liked having him there, liked the way she would find him staring at her when he thought she wasn't looking. It made her heart beat fast and hard, but her mind felt light. His presence distracted her from her worries about striking out as well. Grace was a good catcher but only a middling batter. She walked more often than she managed to get a hit, and she found the prospect of going up to bat nerve wracking.

She could feel him watching her as she removed her padding, and smiled. His attention felt good. It was a stark contrast to the usual feeling of being watched. Grace would definitely get up to bat this inning, so she had to be quick about removing all her catcher's gear so as not to hold up the game. She finished just in time and ran up to the plate. She managed to walk in a run extending their lead.

Grace and her mother went to get the MR results from the neurologist.

"Well, there's nothing out of the ordinary showing up on the scan. That doesn't mean there is nothing there, just that there is nothing obvious. I would suggest removing MSG from Grace's diet and seeing if that makes any difference to the frequency or severity of her headaches." The Dr. tapped his pen against the notes as he spoke.

Grace's mom went through all the food in the house, throwing out anything with monosodium glutamate as an ingredient. Grace sighed internally as the doritos, and salami and all the other goodies went into the trash can, hoping it would at least make a difference.

"I know it's going to be hard, Grace, but we'll find lots of yummy foods that don't have MSG in them, you'll see," her mom said.

The doritos went, but the pounding, relentless headaches did not.

Summer came hot and humid, bringing n relief for Grace at all. This year, she was going to day camp at her school. Every morning, she boarded the crowded bus, just like a normal school day. One day she played dodgeball for the first hour. Grace got hit by the big red ball so hard it knocked the breath straight out of her lungs in a whoosh of air.

"Come on, Grace," yelled one of the boy on her team. She sat on the sideline watching th rest of the game, glad to be out early.

Next up was arts and crafts. Grace began by drawing a green field with a big tree at one end. She was halfway through drawing a jagged stump when she noticed just what she was doin

e crumpled the paper into a ball and tossed it
 the trash, mind suddenly filled with Nathan's
ce a rictus of pain.

 The siren song of the swing set called
t to Grace, and she obeyed, running out and
mping onto the solid, plastic seat. Grace
mped her legs in a rush to get as high as
ssible as quickly as she could. When she felt
r stomach drop she suddenly stopped pumping
d let herself slow down, dragging her feet on
e ground until she finally came to a halt.

 The cavernous school toilets were dark
d crowded with stalls. The old stained tiles
sembled something out of a horror movie, in
ace's estimation. Grace avoided them as much
 she possibly could.

 But twice so far this summer, Grace
d avoided the toilets all day, only to wind
 dancing on her doorstep, trying to hold it
 while she fumbled with her key. Both times
ding in hot urine running down her legs as
e unlocked the door in tears, humiliated and
aid and unable to deal with it all. She couldn't
e another day of rinsing her wet clothes in the
k and ringing them out just to bury them in
 hamper and hope they dried out before her
ther noticed. How would she even explain
self? *Sorry mom, too terrified of imaginary
nsters to pee at school?*

 So Grace sucked it up and headed for
 girl's toilets. They were down a long empty
lway. The fluorescent lighting flickered
onsistently, making the shadows jump and
ce on the walls. There were too many mirrors,
e above each of the four sinks, and there were
e stalls. Grace used the toilet quickly. She
shed it and hurried over to the sink to wash her
ds, keeping her eyes locked on what she was
ng, sure that if she looked into the mirror, the
 would smile back at her from the stall. She
 out of the room, wiping her wet hands off on
 shorts. Grace wished for the thousandth time
t she was one of those girls who had a group
of friends that followed her to the bathroom,
chatting and laughing, without a care in the
world.

 Home wasn't much better. Grace felt
watched from the second she could see her
house, almost like the structure itself was waiting
for her. She grabbed a packet of fruit snacks from
the kitchen and turned on the television. Then she
sat on the couch and waited to hear her mother's
key in the door. It was almost a 2 hour wait every
day. One in which her imagination threatened to
drive her crazy repeatedly. Her eyes would dart
over to the staircase every so often, sure the hag
would be peering at her through the bars. The
only eyes she saw were her cat's.

 Sometimes Grace would stare out her
bedroom window. Just beyond the backyard,
the woods started. They went all the way up
the hill. There was a park at the top, but Grace
never went there. It was more of a place for
teenagers to hang out and smoke and drink, full
of broken glass, with a netless basketball hoop
and a few graffiti covered benches. The trees
always seemed to stare back. Grace told herself
it was just kids out in the woods, being secretive
and doing things their parents wouldn't like, but
it didn't feel that way at all. It felt pointed and
direct, like she had the attention of someone or
something.

 One night, Grace dreamed. The woman
who wasn't quite her mother sat on the couch
and smiled at her, mouth just a little too wide.
*Why don't you go upstairs, Grace, and get a
game for us to play?* Dream Grace didn't want
to go upstairs, but she couldn't stop herself.
Everything slowed down as she took to the
stairs. Detuned piano music filled her ears as she
slowly, painfully took each step. There seemed to
be more steps than she remembered. Too many.
When she finally reached the top, she opened
the closet door. It was full of winter clothes and
board games on a shelf. She grabbed at the first

box she saw and turned to take to the steps again. There seemed to be a hundred of them. At the bottom, the woman who was not her mother waited, smiling. Her teeth shone like daggers, too big for her mouth. Grace stepped down the first stair, and a stale wind rustled through her hair. *Yes, Grace, let's play a game.* The breeze became a hand, and it gripped her hair tightly and pulled her back. *I like games, Grace, don't you?* The wrinkled face of the hag stared down at her, with milky, sightless eyes. Grace woke up screaming.

Her mother, her real mother, stumbled down the hallway and into her room.

"Grace, what's wrong?" Her voice was hoarse with sleepiness.

"I had a nightmare." Grace was sobbing.

"It's okay, baby," her mother sat on her bed and gave her a hug."I'll get you some warm milk, and turn on a light." Grace's mother walked out into the hall and flipped on the light. "I'll just be a minute, and then you can tell me all about it."

Grace sat alone and tried to calm herself. She didn't want to talk about her dream. She hated how real it felt. Why was this happening to her? Grace dried her tears on her blanket and wished she was someone else, someone brave. It was all getting to be too much for her. When would it end?

Grace drank her warm milk and refused to talk about the dream. She couldn't bring herself to describe it. What good would it do? Her mother would be powerless to stop the fear that ate away at everything she did. It was Grace's brain that was the problem. She cried some more, and her mother rubbed her back until she fell into a quiet, dreamless sleep.

The next day Grace scoured the bookcase downstairs until she found a book called Witches and Wizards. It was part of some Time/Life collection that her father's girlfriend had bought, grown bored with, and given to her. She flipped through until she came to a page about Baba Yaga. The illustration looked just like the hag in her dreams. Grace read all about her flying mortar and pestle and her chicken legged hut. She slammed the book closed when she got to the part about her eating children. Her stomach suddenly queasy, Grace grabbed her lunch and her key and headed off to day camp.

The day flew by with Grace playing games and laughing with her friends. But the hag was never far from her thoughts. Soon she was on the bus headed home again. Instead of going inside she walked down to the park and sat on a swing. She swung slowly back and forth, willing the time to pass, hoping someone she knew would come by and chat with her for a while. Anything to keep from going back to the house alone. No one came. After an hour, she gave up and headed home.

Grace walked up the front steps and with a shudder, unlocked the front door. She headed straight to the living room and turned on the television. Soap operas were on, her mother's favorite. She sat on the big couch and waited for her mother to get home, unsure how long she could go on like this, but unable to see a way out. Her fears were overwhelming her, sucking the joy out of her life. Grace longed for the courage she sometimes felt in her dreams, the ones where she was a superhero fighting off the baddies, but in reality she felt small and powerless in the face of her fears. Every day was like a nightmare. She felt as though she lived in a horror movie, and there was only one way it could all end. Grace was unsure if it was possible to actually die from fright, but she was quite sure that she'd be the person to find out, if it was.

Grace sat in the living room watching television as her mother prepared dinner. Afterwards they played a few rounds of Yahtzee, their favorite game to play together. Grace even won a round. Then she went straight in the bath while her mom made popcorn on the stovetop.

Once she was in some fresh pajamas, they sat down with the popcorn to watch a movie. Grace looked through the VCR tapes and settled on The Sword In The Stone. Soon she was lost in the tale, munching handfuls of popcorn and cheering on the heroes in their quest.

After the movie, Grace marched up to bed, her head filled with Madam Mim being outsmarted by Merlin. She turned on her little black and white TV, and promptly fell asleep. In her dream she was asleep in her bed, as the hag crept soundlessly into her room. Her clothes were practically rags, her hair was sparse and stringy and hung past her shoulders. Her arms were long and thin, bony even, with crepey, mottled skin. Dream Grace sat up in her bed.

"What do you want?" she asked the witch.

We want you, girl, and all that you have. The hag smiled, her mouth full of broken teeth. *Your body, your life, Grace.*

Dream Grace lost all her courage then, as the hag drew closer. She opened her mouth to scream. Nothing came out but air. The witch was on her now, pulling her hair, sucking the breath from her. Her milky eyes just inches from Grace's own. Grace felt the others appear in the room, the other mother, who was not quite her own, the burnt man, who she was sure she'd met before, with his claws and his smoke and his angry blue eyes. They huddled around her bed, grabbing at her, their cackles filling her ears. Grace tried to shake herself free, but the hag held her in an iron grip with her nobby, twig like fingers. She looked so frail but she was so much stronger than Grace could have imagined.

Come play with us forever, Grace. Said the other mother, her smile too wide and full of sharp teeth.

Give us your heart. The shadow man raked his claws down Grace's legs, blood welling up in their wake.

Give us your soul, Grace. The hag screeched, her voice taking on an otherworldly quality that Grace had no words for.

Grace thrashed in the hag's arms but it was useless. The old one crouched above her breathing her sickly sweet breath into Grace's face. The other mother smiled at her from over her shoulders.

You're ours now, forever and ever and ever.

The hag's face was contorting. Her jaw unhinged and her mouth gaped wide with jagged yellow teeth. Inside her mouth was a perfect black void, and it was swallowing Grace whole. She screamed but nothing came out. Grace could feel clawing at her chest, where her heart was, but it was all so far away now. All that was left was the cold, inky blackness surrounding her as she was sucked from her own body. There was a titter of laughter, and then there was no more to see. Suddenly she was blown up towards the ceiling, expelled from the witch's lungs in one long, deep exhalation. She was floating above the scene, watching the hag stretch Grace's skin like a balloon and step inside, disappearing into her body. No one seemed to notice her consciousness, floating above, watching. The others receded into the dark, their games ended, and hag Grace sat up in bed, staring at nothing.

Grace was beginning to think this was not a dream. Maybe, just maybe she wasn't mad. Maybe that *thing* was real, had stalked her, and had stolen her body. Normally she woke before anything really happened to her. Grace pressed her essence tightly into the corner of the ceiling. *Make yourself small, do not be seen.* It had worked once before. She had no idea if she was asleep and dreaming or not, but her only advantage was that all her nightmares seemed to believe she was gone. Maybe if they kept believing that, she'd have a chance.

Morning came, and Baba Grace went off to live Grace's life. Disembodied Grace waited until there was no one left in the house, then floated down to look in the mirror. She could just about see herself, a small shimmer, hardly anything at all. How was she supposed to fight for her own body? Why was this happening to her? The main thing that she noticed was that without her body, the fear was gone. But now she felt other things. Anger. Rage. She wanted her life back.

Baba Grace went to camp. Outwardly she seemed normal, if a bit quiet. She kept to herself, played on the swings, dribbled a basketball around and managed to keep herself looking busy. In reality, she was savoring every breath. The feel of the wind through her hair, the warm sun beating down on her face. Her stomach did flips as she swung higher on the swings and she let out a titter of laughter.

She smiled softly as she bit into her lunch. Salami and mustard. What a fine combination. She couldn't remember having this before, but it tasted good and right. Had she ever been real? A human mortal eating sandwiches and playing games in the sun? She reached back into her mind, but there was nothing but a jumble of emotions and images, like shattered glass littering the night. Nothing to make sense of. No way to know who she had been before she was this.

But now, now she was the girl child. What's it? *Grace*. Yes, now *she* is Grace. Now she had these strong legs and these knobby knees to run with and these lungs to breathe air and now she could do anything she wanted. What did she want? What a question! To live. Let us live. Let *me* live. Who are we? We are Grace. Only Grace. I am Grace.

Back at the house, disembodied Grace hung about aimlessly. She was trying to ascertain the rules. What would keep her from floating off into space if there was no ceiling? What even was she? Apparition Grace tried to touch things. She could not. She tried to pet her cat, who hissed and spun around wildly, then ran and hid under her mother's bed. The other nightmares were nowhere to be found, but she'd forgotten them anyway. Time was amorphous. Had it been ten minutes or ten hours? She had no idea.

Then the girl came home.
Wait, that's not quite right. Who am I?
The girl came into the house and went into the kitchen and came out with cheese and crackers. She sat on the sofa eating them while she watched cartoons. This was all wrong. Wron wrong WRONG.

The apparition became substantial in its anger. She rushed to the mirror and noted the darkness, the coldness of its presence. She was still just a flicker, but she *felt* real. She felt righteous. She felt anger boiling up from some unknown well of her being. She flew back into her corner and lurked, her rage simmering.

When night came, the girl child slept. The apparition floated above, trying to remember wl she was there. Everything seemed to not be quit right, but she couldn't remember. Every time sh tried to think, the sense just floated off into the ether. The whos and whys escaped her, leaving her frustrated. The apparition grew tired of watching the girl sleep. She looked comfortable and happy. The apparition's rage churned inside her. She floated out into the hallway and settled at the top of the steps. Here she felt centered. Sl could see in both directions down the hall and down the stairs. Maybe she could fix things, if only she knew what was wrong.

Why didn't she know what was wrong? How long had she been here? Suddenly she was agitated again. *What came before this?* The apparition didn't know. She tried to reach back into her memory, but there was nothing there bu a patchwork of violent images and emotional imprints. Was she trapped? Was she powerless? She would have to find out.

Grace's dreams were odd. People spoke in
language she didn't know. A cabin danced and
run on bird's legs. Grace thought it was funny,
and she laughed. She dreamed of cold air and
deep forests. But she woke to the summer sun
shining through her window. She looked out into
the woods behind her house and felt drawn to
them. Something out there felt right.

Grace got dressed and ready for day camp.
She was excited to have another day to idle away
in the sun with the other children. She wasn't
sure exactly how to talk to them, but that didn't
really seem to matter. She could just enjoy being
near them. It was enough for now.

She sat near the back of the bus by herself
and looked out the window. A girl sat down next
to her. "Hello, Grace. How are you?" The girl
had wavy blonde hair, blue eyes and a smattering
of freckles.

"Oh, hi," Grace searched her brain for
anything. A scrap floated into her focus. "Hi,
Jamie. I'm okay. Just daydreaming, I guess."

Jamie nodded like that was a reasonable
response, and started talking about what she'd
bought in her packed lunch that day. Grace felt
a sense of relief wash over her, like she'd passed
some test she hadn't known she was taking. The
rest of the bus ride was full of aimless childhood
chatter, and Grace felt whole and happy.

It was a good day. She played a game of
basketball with some of the other boys and girls.
She was nervous at first, for some reason, but the
memory of how to play came rushing back. Her
body took over and knew just what to do. Then
they made paper chains in rainbow colors and
hung them up to decorate the lunch room. Grace
found the repetitiveness of the task comforting.
By lunch time the hall was full of decorations
dangling from the walls. Jamie sat nearby
chatting to her and Grace found she liked that
too. It was nice to focus on someone else's words
and thoughts. It took the pressure off of her to
come up with interesting things to say all the
time. Jamie did not seem to mind doing most of
the talking, and the exchanges began to feel more
natural as the day went on.

After lunch the girls played tag with a few
other people, and then they headed over to the
swingset. "I LOVE the swings!" Grace shouted
as she jumped on one.

Jamie laughed, "Me too!" The girls
pumped their legs trying to go as high as they
could. "Do you want to come over to my house
after camp?" Jamie called out.

"I will have to go home first and call my
mother to ask!" Grace called back, laughing.

"Okay!" Jamie said. "I'll come with you
and wait. My mom won't mind, as long as we
don't take too long."

The girls jumped off the swings giggling
and ran out into the big field to sit in the grass
and pick daisies.

"Do you know how to make daisy chains?"
Grace asked. Jamie shook her head, so Grace
showed her how to loop the stems around and
pull. They made each other daisy crowns and ran
around the field laughing. She didn't even notice
the spot where the old tree stump had been.

The girls chatted and giggled the whole
bus ride home. When they got to Grace's house,
she picked up the phone and dialed the office her
mother worked at. She was happy that Grace was
finally playing with other children.

"Come home at five o'clock so I can make
us dinner." her mom said, "and have fun!"

Jamie lived just around the corner from
Grace in a yellow house with a big backyard.
Grace thought Jamie's house was a lot nicer
than hers, even though it had fewer bedrooms
and no upstairs. It was smaller, but something
about it was homey and comforting. Maybe it
was the wood paneling and shag carpet in the
living room. Perhaps it was just the fact that it
wasn't her own home. She couldn't put her finger

on exactly why, but Grace was much happier practically anywhere else.

The girls had cookies and juice and played with dolls while Jamie's mom watched soap operas. It was fun but the time flew by too fast, and suddenly it was five o'clock and time to head home for dinner.

"See you tomorrow, Jamie. Thanks for having me over!"

Grace's mom was making fish sticks when she got in. "Go wash up, Grace, they'll be done in ten minutes." Her mom seemed cheerful, and Grace was happy to see sweet corn and mashed potatoes were also bubbling away on the stove. Dinner smelled great, and she skipped up the stairs to wash her hands.

Grace entered the bathroom and turned on the water. She stuck her hands under the faucet and grabbing the bar of soap, began to scrub. Her eyes flicked up to the mirror and then stopped there. She studied her own face and it somehow felt like a stranger's. Her eyes looked like they'd lived a thousand lifetimes. Grace quickly looked away and turned off the water. She dried her hands and ran downstairs, trying not to wonder why everything seemed so strange at that moment.

Dinner tasted just as good as it smelled. Grace mixed her corn into her mashed potatoes and ate them together, savoring the mingling tastes. She dunked her fish sticks in ketchup like any good 8 year old would, the mild tang of the sauce perfectly complimenting the fishy goodness. Grace liked food better than just about anything, except maybe the swings at school. After dinner she enjoyed some vanilla ice cream with chocolate syrup on top. She stirred it together until the ice cream started to melt.

"Yum, ice cream soup!" She spooned up the swirls of chocolate and vanilla while she watched some random sit-com with her mother. The jokes went over Grace's head, but the laugh track told her when to react, and she soon found herself enjoying the show.

"Okay, Grace, bath time!" her mom said. Grace went upstairs and found her pajamas. She carried them off to the bathroom where her mother was already running the water.

The bath was hot and full of bubbles. Grace sat very still until she was used to the temperature. It was not hot enough to scald, but hot enough to be uncomfortable at first. Then she slowly began to move around, sticking her hand into the bubbles and splashing a bit. The bubbles smelled of artificial sweetness, slightly tangy and fruity, but not like any real fruit Grace had ever eaten. She stuck her face through the bubbles and into the water and blew out to make her own bubbles.

By the time Grace got out, her fingers and toes were wrinkled and the water was going cold. The wrinkles made her stomach tighten. They prickled her mind, like some memory, long forgotten, and haunted her. She put on her pajamas and climbed into bed, hiding her hands under the blanket.

Grace's mother turned the television on to a late night talk show. "Good night, Gracie," she said. Then she turned out the light and left the room, leaving Grace alone to rest.

That night, Grace's dreams were troubled. She dreamed of a man with claw-like fingers. He smelled of burning flesh as he stared out of the corner where the cat's litter box was. He tutted her and put a finger to his lips. She dreamed of a woman with long wavy black hair, with frowning wide lips like a fish. She stood over her staring in judgment. Grace felt strings of guilt pulling at her, but she didn't know why. She tossed and turned and woke several times, staring out into the darkness of her room.

Luckily, it was the weekend. Grace slept late into the morning, making up for her restless night. When she woke she tidied her room, put ll the clothes she found on the floor in the hamper, and placed her books on the bookshelf. Then she got dressed, and brushed her teeth. Her eyes seemed strange looking back at her in the mirror. *What's wrong with me?* She stared into her own eyes searching for the answer. All she saw was more questions.

Grace picked up the sticker book on her dresser and flipped through it. There were smelly stickers inside. She scrunched up her nose at all the different scents emanating from the pages, and closed the book, tossing it in the underutilized trash can.

Grace rinsed out her mouth and washed off her toothbrush. She sighed out a deep breath and headed down the stairs. It was Saturday morning and there were tons of cartoons to choose from.

ABOUT HALFWAY DOWN THE STAIRS, SHE STOPPED. HER STOMACH DROPPED AND A WAVE OF COLD FEAR WASHED OVER HER. THE UNDENIABLE SENSATION OF SOMEONE MALEVOLENT STANDING JUST BEHIND HER, WATCHING. BIDING THEIR TIME. WAITING. WANTING NOTHING SO MUCH AS EVERYTHING GRACE HAD. GRACE TOOK A DEEP BREATH, AND RAN.

END CREDITS

SN Humphreys would like to thank w.p. Quigley for inviting her to join this merry band, and his dedication to getting this all to work time and time again. Lucienne LeBeau for her help and encouragement and brilliance. DS Vernon for all his hard work and for being a kickass managing editor. Madi Quinn for everything she's done to get this issue out there, and for being a kindred spirit in so many ways. The entire *Double Feature* team for being awesomesauce. Mom for always being my biggest cheerleader. And finally, James Humphreys for everything everything everything everything. (If you sang that last four words we're now friends, I don't make the rules)

D.S. Vernon would like to thank his cohorts on this wild issue, S.N. Humphreys and Madi Quinn. S.N. Humphreys is a wonderful co-crime-scene-manager. Madi stepped up to the plate with no hesitation and designed a hell of an issue. Not to mention, fantastic stories from both of you! w.p. Quigley for his guidance, coaching, and dedication. Lucienne LeBeau for such early on encouragement and immediate belief in my abilities. Absolutely everyone in the madhouse that is *Double Feature*. And of course, Jenna Griffin, who put up with my crazy ideas, strange interests, and general all around weird demeanor on a daily basis and still manages to strengthen and support me.

Madi Quinn would like to thank w.p. Quigley for believing in her even when (especially when) she didn't. Shannon Humphreys and DS Vernon for being the very best bosses she's ever had. Cheers to the entire team at *Double Feature* because without you, there simply wouldn't be a *Double Feature* and that would truly suck. Lucienne LeBeau for her steadfast friendship, guidance, and for being the only owner of an signed copy of Madi's last book. Rachel Ensley-Pope for her support since day one. Of course, Mary Stefaniak for her unwavering support of a woman living out her dream.

Coming Soon

Issue #4

I DON'T LIKE MONDAYS

FEATURING

MADI QUINN

"Chef de Cuisine" and "Love of an Unbeating Heart"